Your Lycan or Mine?

MICHELE BARDSLEY

DEDICATION

To my Viking
I love you.

To my BFF Renee
Supernatural Forever

CONTENTS

ACKNOWLEDGMENTS

The fans of the Broken Heart series have driven its success from the beginning. Writing about Broken Heart and its residents is such fun for me. I'm so glad you are all part of my world!

"Please accept this sandwich as a gesture of solidarity."

~Castiel, *Supernatural*

CHAPTER ONE

Las Vegas, Nevada

ASH KNEW SOMEONE was following her.

To get out of the stifling heat and suffocating quiet of the Soul Searchers office, she'd taken an evening walk. Her investigative partner, best friend, and pain-in-the-ass werewolf Sedrick "Nor" North had sashayed his drag queen self down to the Four Queens to flirt with the bartender.

Their office building wasn't far from the recently refurbished downtown. The shops on this particular street were closed, but the window displays and the wrought iron street lamps offered soft light. Well-trimmed trees sprouted from perfect dirt squares, which alternated with big pots of multi-colored flowers. Keeping non-indigenous plants alive in the desert took a lot of work—and water.

She stopped at a shop window, using its reflection to see who or what might be trailing her. Moments passed, and no one appeared around the corner. It seemed as though she was alone. Ash cut her eyes to the right and then to the left. Nothing stirred, not even the Las Vegas wind.

A shiver of foreboding made goose bumps rise on her flesh. Everything was so still. Quiet. The air felt heavy, as though storm brewed just beyond the horizon. She couldn't shake the feeling that she was standing helplessly in that awful silence before the thunder roared and the sky cracked open.

Jittery, Ash turned away from the shop. Forget waiting. She'd draw out the one following her.

She stretched her fingers and cracked her neck as she casually continued her stroll. She was never without weapons. She always carried poisoned knives on the sides of her boots. Every pair she owned had compartments to store the specially made blades. Her Sig Sauer .45 rested in her shoulder holster.

Potent soul-shifter magic coursed through her the same way the blood did in her veins though she tried not to use her magic. Magic was energy and using it drained her faster than relying on fists and feet to combat a foe. She was more likely to throw a punch than she was to delve into her supernatural gifts.

Up ahead, she saw the entrance to an alleyway that she knew led to a dead end. If she could draw in her unwanted companion, she'd have the advantage. Her stalker wouldn't have anywhere to go.

As she passed the alley's entrance, she swerved into it and ran as fast as she could to the very back.

She positioned herself against the brick wall next to a foul-smelling Dumpster, and kept her gaze ahead, waiting.

"C'mon," she muttered. "Show yourself."

She didn't hear footsteps or the rough breathing of someone running. No, she felt the oppressive presence slither into the alleyway. The effluvium was so thick that it nearly suffocated her.

"Ash the Destroyer," hissed a gravelly voice. "Thy death is upon you."

"Says you." Her denial croaked out in a ragged whisper. A force she could not see grabbed her throat and pushed her against the wall.

She kicked and punched, but met no resistance. The thing attacking her had no form. She smelled the sulfur, though, and knew the thing trying to strangle her was demonic. The edges of her vision darkened and she gasped for breath. Her only option was magic. She drew on her power and released it through her fingertips. The blue and white energy struck the invisible foe like a lightning bolt. The creature screamed but did not let go. The pressure on her throat increased.

"Close your eyes," yelled a male voice.

She squeezed her eyes shut. She felt an explosion of powerful energy. The miasma attacked her shattered, and a frustrated screech echoed as the evil released its hold on her.

Ash gulped air and rubbed her raw throat. Her heart pounded furiously, and her hands shook uncontrollably.

"Natasha," said a deep, silky voice. She looked up at the man approaching her. He was dressed in a tailored pinstriped Armani suit. His dark hair was short and cut corporate style. He had the sharp, good looks of a GQ model and the arrogant attitude of an alpha male. His dark eyes reminded her of polished amber.

"Who the hell are you?" she managed in a cracked voice.

"I'm the guy who just saved your life." He looked her over with one eyebrow cocked. "I'm disappointed. I expected more from the infamous soul shifter."

"Yeah?" Unnerved by her brush with the demon and irritated with his tone of voice, she kicked him in the kneecap. He stumbled, and she punched him hard in the solar plexus. He flew backward.

He lay stunned on the ground. She took out her Sig and aimed it at the stranger. "I asked you a question, asshole."

He grinned, not intimated by her at all. "I'm Jarod Dante. Your new boss."

"I don't have a boss." Ash wracked her brain. Why did the name Jarod Dante seem so familiar?

"I know Damian and Kelsey," he said, as though he'd guessed at her thoughts. "I'm a friend to Broken Heart."

Ash remembered now. Jarod was a therianthrope who'd hoped to mate with Kelsey, a Changeling. But Damian, king of the lycanthropes, had accidentally turned her into a werewolf, and they fell in love. Jarod had been left out in the cold, and then he disappeared. Why the hell would he show up to save her and outrageously claim he was her boss?

She watched Jarod climb to his feet. He crossed his arms, which tightened the expensive material and showed off impressive biceps. He made her nerve endings buzz with awareness, and she didn't fucking like it.

"The balance between Light and Dark is teetering," he said. "The Convocation has been resurrected to restore the balance."

The Convocation reborn? *No, thank you.* "Wait. *You're* part of the Convocation?"

"Yes." He shrugged. "I needed something to do with my time."

Jarod was playing his cards close to the vest. Didn't matter. She had no hope that anything would be different from the original incarnation. "You tell the new Convocation to kiss my ass."

"Tempting offer," he said. "It is a delectable ass."

His comment stunned her into silence. Reeling from the unwelcome attraction to the man, she attempted to stride past him.

Jarod grabbed her arm and spun her around to face him. His expression became grave. "Why do you think a demon tried to kill you?"

She yanked her arm from his grip. "Everyone tries to kill me."

"The Vedere psychics have issued a prophecy."

Ash frowned. "About me?"

"About Lilith." He paused. "And you."

"I can't wait to hear this."

"Lilith returns, the world burns. The soul shifter is the only key that ensures the demon is never free."

"Why do they make everything rhyme? It's hard to take their prophecies seriously." She narrowed her gaze. "Is this a job for Convocation? Because the answer is a big, fat no."

"The Convocation isn't asking you for anything, Natasha. Fate is the one coming for you." His gaze gentled and his tone softened. "Remember, when the time comes, you must begin where the first sacrifices were made."

Jarod disappeared. No sparkles. No smoke. Not even a good-bye. He just wasn't there anymore.

Rattled by the demon attack, Jarod Dante's appearance, and the news about Lilith, Ash pushed her hands into the pockets of her pink leather jacket and hurried back to the office.

THE NEXT EVENING, in the dimly lit office of Soul Searchers, Ash leaned over the desk. She peered down at the small, brown paper-wrapped box that she'd found on the doorstep. Ash's name had been scrawled on it, but it had no return address. Though she had her suspicions, she hadn't found any clues about where it had come from or who had dropped it off.

"Did you get me a present?" asked Nor, looking fabulous in his electric-blue mini skirt and white blouse. His stilettos were the same eye-popping color as the skirt. He'd gone for a blond pageboy wig. A faux diamond dotted his cheek. His lips were cherry red, his eye shadow glittery blue.

"Only waitresses in roadside diners and hookers past their prime wear that color of eye shadow," groused Ash.

"Jealous much." Nor blinked at her, oblivious to Ash's worry, and gave her the full effect of his false lashes.

"Did you kill a couple of spiders and glue them to your eyes?"

"Ouch." He put a hand to his heart in mock pain. "Remember who taught you how to deliver the throat-punch-groin-kick combo. These heels can draw blood."

He joined Ash at the desk and looked at the box. "Money?" Nor's voice was hopeful. "Come on, large wad of cash!"

"Bomb," suggested Ash cynically.

He poked it. "It's not ticking."

"Bombs don't have to tick." She batted his hand away. "Maybe it's biological. If we open it ... poof ... poison sprays in our faces." She grabbed her throat and made choking noises.

"You're horrifyingly jaded."

"Only about mysterious packages."

"I say we open it." Nor scooped up the box and shook it like a maraca.

Ash reached for the package, but Nor was nearly a foot taller than her. He held it above her head and laughed.

"You don't know what's in there!" she screeched.

"I will in a minuuuuute." He danced backward, and she aimed her boot at his shin. He darted to the left. "Hey! Don't kick me! I bruise easily, and you'll ruin my perfect legs."

"Okay, okay. You do have pretty good legs." Besides, the damned bomb would've gone off by now. "But you're still a dumbass."

"As long as it's cute, I don't care about the intelligence level of my ass." He tore off the paper, throwing it into a nearby trashcan, and then removed the lid. He stared at the contents, frowning.

"What is it?" she asked.

"Statuary. God, I hate knick-knacks. Especially broken knick-knacks." He handed her the box. "Do you think it's worth anything? Maybe we could sell it to a pawnshop and go to the Four Queens for drinks. It's half-price night at the bar."

"It's always half-price night for you. The bartender wants to get under your skirt."

Nor chuckled. "He's so yummy that I'd let him. Too bad he's not the type to enjoy what's under there."

"The way he flirts with you," she said, looking him up and down, "means he's definitely into what's under there."

The tall, leggy werewolf batted his eyelashes again.

Ash shook her head, hiding a smile, as she took out the statue: a headless lion the color of mustard and formed out of cheap clay. Foreboding washed over her and Ash's stomach clenched. Her adopted parents had an odd statue like this one. Dad was a professor of ancient cultures, and he often traveled the world in pursuit of knowledge. He had a lot of weird objects. The statue had always appeared like a cheap knock-off to her. The garish colors and the rough clay parts looked like the efforts of a kindergartner.

"I've seen this before," she said. "It's supposed to have an owl head and a snake necklace."

"As if it's not gaudy enough," said Nor, horrified.

She tapped the statue. "I think this means we have a job."

"Funny, I don't see a client or his deposit." He looked at Ash. "Remember our new philosophy? You can't pay; we don't play. Cough up the dough or we won't go. If a monster caught is what you wish then you better pass the money dish."

Ash grimaced. "I can't believe you remembered those awful mottos we cooked up. We were drunk,

Nor."

"Doesn't matter. We're running a business, not a charity."

"Jeez! Who's cynical now?" She put the statue on the desk and picked up the box. "You know how this works. It's my calling. It's who I am, not just what I do."

"Penance for the souls you devour?" Nor sighed. "Fine. But being noble doesn't pay the bills or put food in our bellies."

"Or buy booze."

"That too."

"We'll try to scare up a paying gig," said Ash. She removed the tissue paper and shook it out. A square-cut piece of parchment floated free. She snatched it and read the note out loud. "If the portal opens to Lilith's hell, only the eater of souls can break the spell. Find three sacrifices from the soul shifter's heart, 'tis the only way to keep out the dark."

"A threat has been issued in badly written rhyme." Nor eyed the headless lion warily. "Eater of souls is a little dramatic."

"The Vedere psychics and their goddamned prophecies. They love being mysterious and secretive." Ash wondered if Jarod had put the Convocation up to this. She couldn't be sure. The statue might be from the Vederes. Ash sighed, leaning back in her chair. She hadn't told Nor about Jarod yet. She didn't want to freak out her friend. Or, to be honest, acknowledge she had the hots for a dude. Nor would spot her hormone fluctuations from a mile away.

"Why is this shit never easy?" asked Nor.

"If it were easy, everyone would do it." Ash stared

9

at the headless lion. *Remember, when the time comes, you must begin where the first sacrifices were made.* She understood now what Jarod meant. She had to go home to Tulsa. Her heart turned over in her chest. "Before we save the world, I need a drink."

Nor stood up and straightened his dress. "Amen, sistah." He looked at Ash, who sat in the office chair with her feet propped on the desk. He leaned a hip against it, frowning. "We deal with demons all the time. This is Las Vegas. Those scaly bastards love it here. You can practically drown in all the sin. We got this, babycakes."

"Yeah. End of the world stuff. No big deal."

Nor sighed. "Can we get *anyone* to pay us for this gig?"

"What? Saving the entire planet isn't enough for you?"

"The electric company doesn't take global gratitude as payment for a bill that's three months overdue."

The lights flickered. Ash and Nor looked at each other, eyes wide. Then the whole office went dark. The buzzing of the electric appliances, from the computer to the coffee maker, silenced.

In the quiet darkness, Nor said, "Told you so."

CHAPTER TWO

Three days later
Tulsa, Oklahoma

"**I HEARD YOU** killed the last dragon," said the drunk.

Ugh. Was that the only thing that impressed parakind these days? Technically, Ash hadn't taken down Synd by herself. The dark mage was dead, except his soul had been missing. And not because Ash took it. It was gone before she killed him. P.S. She happened to know there were a few dragons left and living happily in Broken Heart, Oklahoma, even though the world thought them gone forever.

"You don't look like much. I could take you."

Ash didn't bother looking up from her drink. She'd been imbibing liquid courage to visit where her childhood died. Where everything died. She did not want to go to a place she'd only revisited in nightmares.

To top off her shitty mood, the moron standing next to her table was either an asshole looking to impress other assholes or he was suicidal. He was certainly three sheets to the wind. At the table behind him, his buddies nudged each other, grinning widely.

Cripes.

The bar was small, dark, and seedy. It smelled like smoke and piss. The vinyl chairs were all duct-taped. The jukebox was broken, so the only noise was chattering voices peppered with laughter. Ash liked it here because the parakind patrons kept to themselves. Most people and creatures knew to leave her alone. Those who didn't end up with broken limbs.

Or worse.

Ash sipped her drink. Idly, she wondered how long the guy's patience would hold. Would he let his testosterone get the better of him? She hoped so. Ash hadn't punched anyone in a couple of days.

"Hey. I'm talking to you," the jerk said, his words slurred.

Ash rolled her eyes. She itched to pull out a dagger and jab it in his temple. Instead, she picked up her drink and finished it off.

Seconds later, Nor returned to the table with two rye whiskeys. His fingernails were painted neon pink, which matched his dress, heels, and wig. His make-up, as usual, was perfect. He was sexy as a man or a woman. His werewolf form wasn't bad, either.

Big, Tall, and Dumb sneered at Nor as he sat down. He crossed his legs and sipped his rye. He looked at Ash. "New beaux?"

"You know me, Nor. Got to beat 'em off with a stick."

"You wanna fight me? I'll fry your ass." The man reached down and grabbed her shoulder.

Ash looked up and met his gaze.

"Shit!" He let go and reared back. "They said you had a..." He trailed off, staring at her.

Diamond gaze. She'd heard it before. The night of her awakening, her eyes had turned such a light gray that they sometimes appeared translucent so that her pupils looked like black dots in orbs of white. It disturbed people—and giving 'em the heebie-jeebies often worked to her advantage.

She looked him over. Tall, buff, dressed in jeans and a biker jacket (idiot), he was a clone of every other blustering paranormal jerk who'd tried to make their bones by kicking her ass.

It never ended well.

For them.

"I ain't scared," he said, regaining his composure. He looked over his shoulder and apparently got a boost of confidence from his jeering friends.

"Go away."

"You saying I'm too tough for you?"

Nor laughed. "Oh, honey. You're adorable."

This was not the reaction the inebriated bully expected. He frowned. "Don't laugh at me, bitch."

Nor bared his teeth and let out a low growl.

Oh, for fuck's sake! This guy had a terminal case of stupidity. Ash looked at her half-finished drink, mourning its loss as she stood up. "Let's get out of here, Nor. I'm bored." She put a twenty on the table. Nor tossed the rest of his drink down the hatch and regally rose to his six and a half feet. With heels, he was six foot eight.

She plucked her pink leather jacket from the back

of the chair. Ash hated to be a cliché—an assassin who strode around in leather, but hell, she loved her tailored jacket. Not only was it stylish, but it also had useful magical properties.

"You running away?" Stupid yelled. "That's right. You ain't shit."

Ash turned, pointed at him and released a tiny fraction of her power. Blue and white lights danced around her fingertip. "If you want to keep your soul, asshole, walk away."

The man's eyes widened.

Ash lifted an eyebrow and flicked the magic at him.

He yelped and turned, stumbling back toward his now silent friends.

Nor looped his arm through Ash's. "Well, that was fun."

NOR WENT TO the nearby liquor store to pick up a decent bottle of bourbon. So, Ash had walked to the motel by herself. Since the bar shared the same parking lot, it only took about five minutes to reach the outdoor staircase that led to the second floor. She took the steps two at a time, rusted metal creaking in protest.

This joint was so ancient and so broken down that the owners hadn't bothered switching to a card-key system. She liked the old-fashioned brass key rattling in the lock.

A swish of magical energy warned her she was no longer alone.

She leaned her forehead against the door. Paint flaked off and drifted to the concrete. "I'm so not in the mood to kill you."

"I'm not in the mood to die."

Ash looked up. Jarod leaned against the concrete wall, looking at her, his dark eyes hiding his secrets.

But not his desires.

Ash unlocked the door and swung it open. "Go away." She went into the room and flicked on the light. It cast a dim, yellow glow from the single bulb dangling from the ceiling.

The room didn't boast any amenities. Hell, not even the antiquated television sitting on the dresser worked. The twin beds were hard as rocks. The chair in the corner had stuffing popping out of several tears.

"Wow. What did you ask for? The hobo special?"

"I prefer low key." Ash took off her jacket and tossed it onto the bed.

Jarod's gaze wandered over her black, skin-tight pants tucked into sturdy black boots and her pink tank top. His lazy examination sent electric shivers across her skin.

"I recognize Bernie's work. Not many people get to wear his creations." His gaze flicked to the jacket. "Did he make that, too?"

Ash shrugged. Jarod had a keen eye. Her friend and literal fashion wizard Bernie made all of Ash's clothes. He knew how to make magical materials that wouldn't cut, burn, tear, or restrict. The jacket was one-of-a-kind. It had a dozen pockets. She could hide anything, huge or tiny, in them. They all offered endless storage, and the cloth stretched to accommodate just about any object.

Ash crawled on the bed, leaning against the cheap headboard and stretched out her legs. "What do you want?"

"I'm checking on you."

"You mean you're checking to see if I'm doing what the Convocation wants."

"Convocation 2.0 isn't so bad," he said as he sat on the bed opposite of hers.

Most parakind were terrified of her. Nobody who liked living was completely unafraid of Ash. It was one thing to die. It was quite another to have your essence stolen and stored inside a being with the ability to assume your form. For creatures unfortunate enough to be absorbed by Ash, there was no afterlife.

Ash felt a flicker of guilt, but it did no good to feel sorry about what came naturally to her. Working for the Convocation meant maintaining the balance both ways. Whoever the Convocation marked, she'd taken their souls—good or bad.

She didn't do that anymore.

Most people born on the Earth got to choose what kind of lives they had. They went to school or traveled or took jobs and raised families. They worried about things like love and happiness and loss and sorrow. But for Ash, there was never a choice. Sometimes, you were born into your destiny.

She couldn't change the fact that she was a soul shifter. But only she got to decide how to live her life. Ash would never have a family or a husband or a nine-to-five job. She would never be normal, never be anything other than what she'd been born. But how she used her gift was her choice and hers alone.

Jarod seemed content in the silence and in a weak moment, she allowed herself to think that he was kinda cute.

The door flew open. Nor posed in the doorway,

holding a liter of Buffalo Trace in one hand and a bag of ice in the other. "I'm ba-ack!" He looked at Jarod and grinned, obviously delighted. "Oooh. You brought me eye candy." He lifted the bourbon. "Drink?"

"None for me, thanks," said Jarod.

Ash held up two fingers. "I'll have a double."

Nor strode to the dresser and unwrapped the flimsy plastic cups provided by the motel. A couple minutes later, he handed a cup to Ash. "It's a triple." He took his drink and sat next to the soul shifter. "Who's the yum?" Nor asked. He crossed his legs and looked at Jarod critically. Then he sighed dramatically. "Straight. Too bad." He waved his manicured hand around. "I guess you can have him, Ash."

"Gee, thanks."

Nor's eyes widened and he gasped. "Is he a client? Oh please, please, please let him be a paying client!"

"He's not a client," said Ash. "Unfortunately, he's a minion of the new Convocation."

"I'm not a minion," protested Jarod.

"The Convocation?" Nor pointed at Jarod. "We don't like those uppity bitches. You're not here to recruit my BFF again, are you?"

"No." He turned his gaze to Ash. "I know you received the lion's body."

"Because you sent it."

He shook his head. "Not me. But I do know it's a statue dedicated to Lilith. Lion body. Owl head. Snake necklace."

"Do you know about the bad poetry we received with the headless beast?" Nor sipped his bourbon. "Apparently, my girl is the only one who can keep the demon Lilith from destroying the world."

"I know about the prophecy." He stared at Nor until the werewolf popped up and said, "I need more...um, ice. I'll be back."

Nor left the room, and Ash looked at Jarod. "Subtle."

Jarod moved to her bed and put her booted feet on his lap. She eyed him suspiciously. He pulled off her boots and her thick socks, and then pushed up her pant legs and starting massaging her feet and calves.

"What are you doing?" Whoa. His strong, warm hands against her tension-filled muscles felt so good. The stiffness of stress started to drain and contentment curled in her belly. It would be stupid to give up a free massage just because she didn't want to be attracted to Jarod. Or so she told herself. She enjoyed his touch, and her body hummed with anticipation.

"You want me," he said.

"Said the arrogant therianthrope."

He laughed. "I want you, too."

Why lie? "Yeah, okay. We got sparks, but so what?"

He stopped his excellent massage. She bit back a protest. He stood up and offered her his hand. She looked up at him, feeling lazy. One eyebrow winged upward. He wiggled his fingers and with a huge sigh, she clasped his hand and he pulled her to her feet. He plucked the cup from her grasp and placed it on the rickety nightstand.

"Natasha."

"My name is Ash."

"Not to me."

"Whatever." Ash's gaze dipped to his luscious

mouth. Oh, she shouldn't be looking at him like that. And her heart shouldn't thunder in her chest. And she shouldn't be even the teeniest bit attracted to him.

"You know, most humans aren't as stubborn as you are."

"I'm not human."

"But you are a woman," he said, leaning down to nuzzle her neck. "And I'm a man."

"I'm so glad we've clarified our genders." Ash figured she should pull out of his embrace. Then punch him for daring to assume she'd even consider sleeping with him. It had been a while since she'd been with anyone. Rare was the man who kept her interest. Besides, she tended to terrify most red-blooded males.

Somehow, she knew that Jarod would be the kind of man she'd never get enough of … the kind of guy that would never want to tame her, but could match her in every way. Oh, shit. She was in trouble with a capital T.

"I see your dilemma," he said, lifting his head to stare at her. "You can't decide if you want to kill me … or kiss me."

"Kill you," she whispered. "Definitely."

His lips pulled into a wicked grin. "You could try."

"Maybe I will," Ash said breathlessly, her lips within tantalizing reach of Jarod's.

The first brush of his lips was electric.

Sparks? More like nuclear explosion. Her whole body went molten. She gave in to her lust, returning his kiss with fervor, drawing him closer, wanting more.

Ash broke the kiss. She didn't let go of him—she might collapse if she did. "What are we doing?"

"Having fun. Are you going to say I caught you in a weak moment?"

A whirlwind of emotions claimed her. She tried to sort through them and pick one to flail him with.

"You regret it. You never want it to happen again. I should take a flying leap." His fingers stroked the small of her back in contradiction to his words.

"Do you need me to participate in the conversation?" asked Ash, the chill of her reluctance thawing with his every touch. He brushed a tender kiss on her lips. She melted completely. This was so not like her. She blew out a breath. "We shouldn't do this ... whatever this is."

Jarod pulled back and looked at her. "We're perfect for each other, you know."

"That's only possible if you don't have a soul. When I get the munchies somebody dies."

"You can't take my soul, Natasha. I'm a therianthrope."

She frowned. "So?"

"I'm the last of my kind, just as you are. I'm the one creature on this earth whose soul will never be yours."

"How is that possible?"

"Turns out therianthropes and soul-shifters have a mating history. Did you know soul shifters were only female?"

Ash reared back. "What?"

"Soul shifters needed mates immune to their peculiar hunger."

"Therianthropes."

"Yes. It makes sense. You and I both can change forms. Granted my way is easier because my DNA is malleable."

"So now we're destined mates?" She pulled away and put distance between them. "One kiss doesn't mean we're gonna get married."

Jarod laughed. "Relax, Natasha. I promise not to drag you down the aisle."

Ash noticed he didn't deny his belief that they were mates. She didn't know what stunned her more: The fact he'd suggested it or the fact she didn't hate the idea.

"I have work to do." Flustered, she grabbed her boots off the floor and started to yank them on.

"Are you sure you want to face the past alone?"

She didn't bother asking how he knew why she was here. After all, he'd sent her this direction with all that talk of remembering where the first sacrifices were made.

"You really think my parents' deaths are because of Lilith? That she knew I was the one who could keep her bound?"

"Yes," he murmured. "They had you, the statue, and the prophecy. The problem is that Lilith struck before they could prepare you. And then the Convocation scooped you up."

"Yeah. And what a joy that turned out to be."

Jarod stepped closer to her and cupped her face. His concerned gaze met hers. "Do you need back-up?"

"I have to do this alone," said Ash. "I'm not even taking Nor."

"If you need me..." He trailed off, his gaze filled with genuine concern.

"Yeah," she said, uncomfortable with his obvious worry for her. "Thanks."

CHAPTER THREE

Marietta, Ohio

CLAIRE GLASS WANDERED among the garage-sale treasures. She touched votive candles, potholders, Matchbox cars, and a cookbook. Her fingertips relayed the differences in textures. Smooth. Soft. Bumpy. She could see the sizes and shapes of the items.

The colors were missing.

Gray permeated her once vibrant world. How she longed to see a red rose, a blue sky, and a green Starbuck's logo. Had it been only a year since every happy thing in her life had been stolen? The man she loved. The wedding they'd planned. The new promotion she'd gotten. Hmph. Difficult to be an interior designer without the ability to see color. Even their dream house, which they'd only moved into the week before the accident, had been taken.

Without Henry or her job, she hadn't been able to afford the mortgage payments. Now, she lived in a tiny apartment trying to make ends meet with disability and Henry's life insurance money.

When she'd come out of the coma, the doctors told her that her cerebral cortex had been damaged. Cerebral achromatopsia was the result. She was lucky to be alive and luckier still that only her limited vision was the price paid for the same wreck that took Henry's life.

Snap out of it, girl. Pity parties are so lame. Claire rounded the corner of the table and looked at the items displayed on a rickety bookshelf. Her fingers danced along an assortment of Precious Moments figurines. She knew why she was so damned mopey. Today would've been her first wedding anniversary. Had Henry lived, they would be celebrating, maybe even taking the first step toward starting a family.

Her gaze swept the driveway, looking at the careless displays of toys, shoes, and tools. What the—

Heart thumping, Claire leaned down and reached into the cardboard box labeled "Miscellaneous ~ 25¢ each." The owl head was as wide as her hand and looked familiar. She could see groves in the neck where the head connected to another piece. It was a shame it wasn't intact, but the broken statuary was still extraordinary.

She saw its color.

The owl head was a brilliant red. Claire looked around. If she could see color again, maybe her vision was getting better. What did doctors know? Miracles happened every day.

As her eager gaze bounced around the

neighborhood -- staring at cars, at people, at lawns, she saw the dreary grayness she always did. She looked at the owl head again. For some odd reason, she only saw this object in color.

She stared at it, searching her memory. Where had she seen this before?

Natasha's house.

Her best friend in junior high, Natasha Nelson, had shown her the odd statue during a sleepover. It had an owl head, a lion body, and a snake necklace. Natasha's father studied ancient cultures and supposedly he'd found it on some kind of dig in Israel.

Just before Claire's sophomore year in high school, her father took a new job, and the family moved to Ohio. She hadn't seen or heard from Natasha in years.

She chuckled. This could not possibly be the same owl's head.

What did it matter? She had proof that her vision was healing. Grinning like a lottery winner, Claire dug out her wallet and extracted a quarter.

Finding this little guy was like getting a message from Henry. I'll always take care of you, Claire. Always. That had been the promise he reiterated every day of their lives together. It felt like the statue was his gift to her; a reminder that he was still keeping that promise.

Tulsa, Oklahoma

AFTER SEEING NOR off at the airport, Ash had gone straight to her old neighborhood. She pulled into the gravel driveway and let the rental car idle.

The house was abandoned, the yard unkempt, and the metal fence rusted and broken. Honeysuckle bushes were thick around the listing gate. In the backyard, weeds poked up through the high grass. Somewhere in that mess were the remains of her terrier's doghouse.

Her gaze wandered over the dilapidated house. The Convocation had purchased it and given it to her. She'd let the place fall to rot and ruin because the idea of coming back sent panic crashing through her.

Were the answers to stopping Lilith actually in there? And how could her adopted parents' murders be related to what was happening now?

She felt frozen to the spot. Here was where her life had ended. A rebellious sixteen-year-old, she'd snuck out to go to a party and returned home to find her family murdered.

Ash tasted bile at the back of her throat. She'd never been back to Tulsa since the tragic loss of her family, much less this neighborhood. The only time she even thought about Oklahoma was when she popped into Broken Heart.

That awful night when she lost her parents and the Convocation rescued her, she was taken from the human world and thrust into the paranormal one. She wasn't allowed to do anything but train. Weapons. Martial arts. Magic rites. Learning how to kick ass had given her focus, a way to work out her grief and her rage. Her first jobs had short leashes held by iron-fisted chaperones. After a while, the Convocation trusted her to go into the world, to do her job, on her own.

Ash shut off the car's engine and shoved the passenger door open. What had she hoped to find here? Answers? Redemption? Hope?

She rounded the front of the car and walked to the gate. It was falling off its hinges. Honeysuckle wound through metal loops, reaching toward her like victims reciting last prayers. The sweet scent of the flowers made her nauseous. Staring at them, she drifted back to that night so long ago...

The sweet scent of honeysuckle wafted from the vines entwining the metal fence. She leaned down and tugged off a yellow blossom. Gently she pinched the stamen and withdrew it, licking away the pearl of nectar on its end.

Her mother had taught her how to do that.

Guilt crimped her stomach. She looked at the desecrated flower and wished she hadn't plucked it, hadn't stolen its honey. The yellow petals were already browning and curling inward. Sighing, she tossed it to the ground.

"That house is haunted."

Ash whirled around whipping out her hip daggers. The poisoned tips of the blades hovered above the head of the one who'd crept up on her.

"Are those real?" The little girl's sky-blue eyes were as wide as saucers. "Can I touch one?"

"No." Ash slid the daggers into their holsters. "Don't you know that sneaking up on people can get you killed?"

"It hasn't yet." The girl was dressed in overalls and a yellow shirt. Her feet were bare. Her brown hair was a rat's nest with twigs sticking out of it. The overalls were dirty, too. Cobwebs stuck to her shoulders. "You gonna buy that house?"

"No." Ash looked her over speculatively. "What were you doing in there?"

"I'm not allowed inside."

It wasn't a denial. Well, goddamn. Ash was trying to work up the nerve to go inside the home she'd lived in for nearly sixteen years and this little sprite had explored it already. She made Ash feel like a coward.

"I bet you're not afraid of anything," said the girl.

"You'd lose that bet." Ash stuck out her hand. "Call me Ash."

"That's a weird name." She grabbed Ash's hand and pumped it. "Margaret Lynne Huntson."

Huntson? Looked like her past knew she was arriving and had thrown a party. "Is your father named Rick?"

"Yes. Do you know him?"

He almost kissed me. I almost fell in love with him. "No," she said. "I don't know your daddy. I'm a good guesser."

Margaret Lynne Huntson considered this possibility. Then she peered up Ash suspiciously. "What's my mommy's name?"

"Maggie?"

Margaret's gaze re-evaluated Ash's intelligence. "You're not a good guesser. You're just lucky."

Wrong again, kid.

"My birthday was yesterday," confided Margaret. "I'm officially eight years old."

"That's fascinating. Hey! Isn't it almost dinner time?"

"Nope. You look like my Rock n' Roll Barbie, only she has better hair."

"Oh, yeah? Have you looked in the mirror lately?"

But Margaret was bored with hairstyle insults. She chewed on her thumb. "What're you doing here?"

27

Oh, for the love of humanity. Why couldn't this kid just go away? "Ever hear of the Ghostbusters?"

"Ghostbusters don't wear pink."

"I do." Ash squatted down and got eye-to-eye with her. "Do you know why this house is haunted?"

The girl's eyes flickered. Once again, Ash felt like she was being judged. "Daddy says a girl lived here. Her name was Natasha. A bad man killed her parents and took her away." She tilted her head. Dirt was smeared under her chin. "Do you think he killed Natasha, too?"

"Yes," said Ash. "He did."

"No, he didn't." Her declaration startled Ash. "So, are you gonna talk to the ghost lady?"

"What lady?"

"She's in there. She calls me Tashie. I don't think she's mean," said Margaret. "Just sad." She ran to the fence and pulled off a honeysuckle blossom. "Hey, do you know how to get the honey?"

Ash's stomach squeezed. "Why don't you show me?"

"You just take this part out, very carefully." Margaret gently tugged the stamen out and showed it to Ash. "Then you lick it." Her little pink tongue darted across the fuzzy end. "Do you want to try?"

"Maybe later."

Margaret rolled her eyes. "That's what grown-ups say when they mean no." She tossed the flower to the ground. "I gotta go home now."

Ash watched her run down the driveway and wondered how her bare feet could take the biting abuse of the gravel. She crossed the street and pivoted right, skipping down the sidewalk.

She was going in the direction of Rick's old house.

Three blocks up, two blocks to the right, and one block left. Did he still live there? Or had he just moved into the same neighborhood? Oh, hell. Why did she care?

Her gaze caught the discarded flower. Then she looked at the house.

It was time to face her ghosts.

CHAPTER FOUR

THE FURNITURE WAS gone. Ash didn't know why she thought it would all be here, dusty and disused maybe, but in place. In some part of her mind, she'd believed everything would be the same. Ash had wanted her memories to stay intact. She wanted confirmation that she had once been normal, sane.

But there was nothing here.

Just an empty house.

Still, she hesitated outside her parents' bedroom. For a long moment, she stared at nothing, preparing her mind for the worst. Then she pushed open the door.

Late afternoon light filtered through the double windows on the right side of the room. From there, she could see the porch and the high grass of the front yard.

She felt nothing.

All the same, she edged to the left and opened the closet door. Empty. Like the room. Like the house. Like her heart.

No, not her heart. Jarod's image flashed through her mind, and she knew he'd come to her if she only asked. And how could she discount Nor and her friends in Broken Heart? She might've been a loner once, but no longer.

Her adrenaline spiked as she walked to the center of the room and let her gaze take in the space. There was no evidence of the violence. The carpet and padding had been discarded, leaving only the scarred and stained wood floor.

For more than a decade, Ash had taken the awful memories out and examined them often over the years. The horror framed those moments like flaking gilt. But standing here now where the worst moment in her life occurred, the pain was nearly crippling.

Memories of that night floated through her mind. They scalded her even now…

Blood. On them, on the bed, on Tashie's hands. She screamed and backed away, trying to process the horror. No, no, it wasn't true. Her eyes were playing tricks on her.

"Jack?" She stumbled forward and reached out to her terrier. She wanted to grab him, wanted to drag him away from the carnage, but he felt wrong. Like a toy that had lost its stuffing.

He was dead, too.

Someone had killed her dog. Someone had killed her parents. She fell to her knees and emptied her stomach. The fermented smell of vomit mixed with the awful rusted scent of blood.

She greedily sucked in oxygen as tears squeezed from her

31

eyes. Bile rose in her throat, and she tasted yeasty-sour beer. For a second, she thought she would puke again.

"Destroyer."

She rolled onto her side and stared up at the thin creature with its round head and stick-like limbs. His eyes were red, his skin green, and his clothes tattered. He smelled like mold. He looked like death.

Her death.

"My queen said I could eat you, but you were not here," he said in an incredibly beautiful voice—an angel's voice that did not match his devil's body. "So, I had a snack. Your mother tasted especially delicious—as I imagine you will taste."

"Get away from me!" She tried to kick at him, but he merely laughed. He bent down and grabbed her by the throat, lifting her easily as if she weighed nothing. She flailed, trying to strike him with hands and feet.

"You do not look like much," he said. "She should not be afraid of you."

What was he talking about? And why had he called her Destroyer?

"Your death will please my queen, and she will repay my deed with all that I desire."

With his hand squeezing the breath out of her, she couldn't scream. Her limbs grew too heavy to move.

"Look at me, Destroyer."

She lifted her eyes to his monster gaze. Her stomach cramped so painfully, she opened her mouth to cry out. Only a rasp escaped. The pain throbbed through her unmercifully. Every nerve ending felt on fire.

She could not break the stare of the creature holding her.

The pain welded her to the creature. She felt ... connected. Now, she felt his shock, the coldness of his flesh, the fetid breath in his wizened lungs, and the double beats of two hearts.

Blue and white lights erupted from her skin. Tendrils

elongated and stretched, wrapping around him.

"No!" he shouted. "No!"

Tashie felt as though she had shouted the words. She was fused to him. His evil tasted as horrid as the bile crowding her throat.

The beams glowed brighter and brighter. Through her terror and her graying vision, Tashie saw a strange, red radiance pulsing like a heartbeat. The small luminous globe radiated in the center of his being. It was so pretty. So warm. So alive.

She reached for it. Not with her hands, but with her mind. She plucked it from him as if she were picking a ripe apple from an old tree.

He released her. She collapsed to the floor, inhaling in shaky breaths. She felt electrified.

Her gaze landed on the heap lying a foot away.

Tashie crawled to where the monster had fallen. She gripped a shoe and yanked, but there was no need. It was no longer attached to anything. Just like her. No longer attached to anything.

Tashie was gone, and Ash was born.

She'd earned the title Destroyer during her years with the Convocation. Ash had never, ever taken the form of the ghoul. That was the one soul she'd never regretted eating. Now she understood his references to the queen and knew he spoke of Lilith.

Was it possible that the demon had known Ash would one day be the key to keeping her locked in hell? After all, Ash did play a part in Lilith's original banishment, though it was the vampire Phoebe and her half-demon mate Connor who ultimately vanquished the female demon.

Ash checked the rest of rooms, saving hers for last. It was stupid to walk around and remember. Her parents had loved her. And the last words they'd ever heard from her was: *I hate you.* They said she couldn't go to Rick Huntson's party. Only she defied them and went anyway. Guilt squeezed her stomach again. The loss of her family was a heavier burden than any other she carried.

Ash walked into the kitchen, which no longer had its appliances. The counters were filthy. The wallpaper hung in tattered strips. The linoleum floor cracked and peeled with years of neglect.

She entered her bedroom and paused.

Even without her bed and desk, it was smaller than she remembered. Dust exploded from the brown carpet with every step she took. And there to the left of her bed, the infamous window—the one she had used to sneak out. If only she hadn't ... maybe she could've saved her parents.

As she walked toward it, she felt the release of magic. Her hip daggers came out automatically, and she spun around in a circle.

"Tashie." Heart pounding, she looked to her right and saw her mother—or rather a green-edged reproduction. The visage of her mom stood near the window, hands clasped in front her, her eyes focused straight ahead.

A spell. Of course her parents would know about magic and parakind. They'd kept their secrets so well. She wondered if she'd never been attacked by the ghoul and imbibed her first soul if she could've lived a normal life. She couldn't comprehend being anything other than what she was. Wishing for things that could never be was a waste of energy.

Ash looked down and saw her feet encased in a green glow. She'd stepped on the trigger. It worked the same as pushing a button on an answering machine. When you pressed it, the message appeared.

"Obviously, your father and I are dead."

Pragmatic to the core, Mom. Ash smiled fondly and tried to pretend that she didn't feel as if she'd taken a sword blow to the gut.

"We tried to give you a normal life, but we tried to protect you, too. Maybe too much. We wanted to tell you about your powers when you turned eighteen. If you're watching this, then it's too late for any of that. You probably know about the Vedere prophecy and about keeping Lilith locked away from the earthly plane. At least we can help you there.

"We separated the statue into three pieces to make it difficult for Lilith to find. There must be three sacrifices, and once blood has been spilled in Lilith's name, the statue made whole will become Lilith's vessel. She will be free, and our world will die."

Mom paused. She cleared her throat. "Go to the attic. In the back right corner, you'll see a board that doesn't quite match the others. Underneath it is a box that contains the snake necklace. Good luck, sweetheart."

Her mother looked to the right and then Ash's father appeared. With his receding hairline and thick glasses, he looked like an absent-minded professor— which, of course, he'd been.

He smiled and waved. "We love you, Tashie. Please know that no matter what passed between us, we loved you more than our own lives."

He placed his arm around Mom right before their images flickered and disappeared.

Ash stared at the empty space. Too late. She'd gotten their message too late. Not long after she'd killed the ghoul, the Convocation rescued her. She awoke in their facility, disoriented and frightened.

Ash stepped back and then forward again. She jumped up and down. It was no use. The magic had dissolved. Her parents were gone. She squelched the rising need to weep. No! She had shed her tears. She'd learned to control her emotions. Emotions made her weak, made her lose focus. *Heart of stone, mind of steel.* That had been her mantra for ten years.

Frowning, Ash examined the room. Usually such spells were cast so that only the person for whom the message was intended could trigger it. Once delivered, the magic dissipated.

So how the hell had Margaret Lynne Huntson activated the message meant for Ash?

With this thought circling, she went to the hallway and pulled on the rope that opened the hatch. The ladder unfolded from the door and she climbed into the dust-filled attic. There were no windows up here, no light. Ash whispered a glow-spell and white sparkles filtered into the small, dark space.

She hurried to the right side. Finding the board was easy because it had already been removed.

The box was gone.

CHAPTER FIVE

WHEN ASH ZIPPED the sedan into the driveway of Rick Huntson's house, she saw red smoke billowing out from the shattered front windows.

She got out of the car and ran up the clean-swept walkway. The door had been torn off, so it was easy to get inside.

The stink of sulfur nearly knocked her on her ass. She could see through the smoke, but the dark magic was another matter. Sorcery thickened the air. She could almost breathe it.

Goddamn it. The demons must've sensed the snake necklace. Whatever protections her parents had put on it to keep it hidden for all these years dissipated the moment Margaret took the necklace from the house.

"Ash the Destroyer."

The voices came from nowhere. From everywhere. Dread filled her. Demons.

"Leave, assholes." She sent the command booming through the house.

The evil bastards laughed. "We do not serve you."

Ash closed her eyes and delved into her inner being. The souls she'd consumed over the years swirled together, long strands of color that fluttered like ribbons tossed by the wind. She chose Ealga, who had been an Irish witch directly descended from a Celtic goddess.

Imbibing a soul meant taking the personality, the form, the memories, the skills, the magic, and hell, even the clothing. Her clothes became part of her as she morphed, and when she assumed a new form, she was dressed in whatever clothing the souls had died in.

The transformation took precious minutes. Soul-shifting wasn't like putting on a costume. She had to combine herself with the other, weaving the two of them together until they were bound. That was only the first part. The second was the re-forming of her body as it morphed to match the other's shape.

As Ealga, she grew taller, her limbs more graceful, her body lithe as a dancer's. She wore a diaphanous blue gown. Her long, black hair was braided. She was also barefoot.

Ash opened her eyes and saw the situation not only from her perspective but also from Ealga's.

The witch knew what to do. She raised her pale, thin arms and muttered a long incantation. Ash didn't understand the words, but she got their meaning.

White light exploded from her palms, expelling the smoke, the dark magic, and the sulfur. The demons screeched like whipped bitches.

Their malicious presence disappeared.

"We sense a child." Ash-Ealga ran up the stairs. She opened the door to the left. Here was a little girl's room—with its pink walls and stuffed animals and scattered books.

She bent low and lifted the bed skirt. Margaret lay pressed against the carpet, her eyes wide and her body trembling. She'd had a bath and was dressed in purple pajamas.

"Ash!" She scrambled out and threw herself into Ash-Ealga's arms.

Shocked, she tried to hold on to the wiggling mass of Margaret Lynne Huntson as she staggered to her feet. "How do you recognize us?"

"What do you mean?" Margaret's tear-stained face lifted just long enough to study Ash-Ealga. "You look like you."

She didn't have time to ponder Margaret's incredible statement. "We must go. Where is the box?"

"What box?" she asked, sniffling.

"Do not lie, child."

"I hid it in my closet."

Carrying the trembling little girl, Ash-Eagla hurried to look. On the top shelf was an intricately carved black box, which she grabbed. She gave it to Margaret to hold.

"I didn't open it."

"Only because you didn't know how." Ash-Eagla hurried down the stairs.

"Where's my mommy and daddy?"

"We sense no others."

"They're in the kitchen! We can't leave without

them."

She put Margaret down in the foyer. "Go to the car. We will find your parents."

As soon as the girl ran toward the sedan, Ash-Eagla hurried to the kitchen. Food and broken dishes littered the floor. The smell of garlic and marinara sauce filtered through the rusty scent of blood.

Margaret's mother was pinned to the refrigerator by the broad, sharp blades of a butcher knives. Her unseeing brown eyes accused the soul shifter of being too late.

"The second sacrifice," said Ash-Eagla. "Her blood belongs to Lilith."

"Natasha!"

Ash-Eagla turned. Jarod Dante stood in the doorway, his silver staff at the ready. "What do you need?"

"Protect the child and the box she carries."

He nodded and disappeared.

Rick Huntson lay facedown on the floor, covered in spaghetti noodles. The red spattering his clothes was not sauce. Gently, Ash-Eagla rolled him over.

Stab wounds covered his chest. His T-shirt was tattered and stained. He was an older version of the boy Ash had known. Still handsome with careless brown hair and slanted cheeks and that dip in his chin.

Ash-Eagla could see the residual soul of Rick Huntson. Unlike his wife, he was still tethered to his body. She laid her hands on his chest.

"We ask the Goddess for Her blessing. Heal this warrior, this father, this husband. Give him his life so that he may serve You and others, our Holy Mother, Creator of All Life, Bringer of All Healing."

Energy emanated from her palms, basking Rick's body in a gold glow. His wounds sealed shut. His breath returned. The soul so close to leaving its host now settled with purpose into his chest.

Rick groaned and his eyes fluttered open. "Mag Pie."

"Margaret is safe."

He seemed to comprehend that his wife wasn't. Perhaps he had been spared seeing her murdered, which meant she had seen him attacked. Her last thoughts must have been about her husband and daughter.

Rick's eyes closed again, and he slid into unconsciousness.

Ash moved away. She knelt, took a deep breath, and stripped herself free of Eagla. Removing a soul felt like having her skin peeled from her muscles and her muscles torn from her bones. Souls could be coaxed into becoming one with her, but none of them liked going back into the mental limbo.

She screamed—she always screamed—as the soul ripped free of its binding and returned to its place within her psychic core.

After several moments of deep breathing, Ash climbed unsteadily to her feet. She refused to panic, but she felt a crazed sense of urgency.

In the dining room, she took off the tablecloth, uncaring about the dishes and glasses that clattered to the carpet. She returned to the kitchen, spread the cloth, and rolled Rick onto it. She tied one end around his feet then grabbed the corners of the other end and dragged him from the house. The stairs weren't fun to navigate and the cloth snagged on the sidewalk.

Then Jarod was there, picking up the unconscious man and striding to the car. The driver's side door opened. Margaret popped out, still clutching the precious container.

"Daddy!"

"Open the back door," directed Ash.

Margaret did as she asked and watched as Jarod placed Rick into the back seat.

She shut the doors. She was sweating now, from exertion and fear. "Get in the car, kiddo."

Margaret looked at her with wide blue eyes. "Is he dead?"

"No."

"Is Mommy?"

"Yes," said Ash. "Get your ass in the car."

Margaret did not burst into tears. Instead, she climbed into the driver's side, scooted across the gearshift, and sat silently in the passenger seat.

"They'll be safe in Broken Heart," said Jarod.

"I'll drive straight there. Let them know I'm on the way with refugees. Take the necklace with you."

He nodded, and then he cupped her face and kissed her hard. "Be careful."

He took the box from Margaret and flickered out.

Ash opened her jacket and withdrew a black ball about the size of an orange from her pocket. She re-entered the house and placed the ball in the foyer. Standing out in the yard, she put her palms out and shouted, *"Eradico!"*

Ash could harness magic, but for powerful spells such as this one she used triggers, such as the black ball, to keep from draining her own energy.

The house erupted into flames. Within moments, it would be reduced to soot. No bodies would be found. The family would be assumed dead. Neighbors would call 9-1-1, but fire trucks would be too late. Since the fire was magic, it would not spread. It would do its job and disappear.

Ash returned to her old house and parked by the curb, leaving the engine running. She needed to get the hell out of the neighborhood, but damn it, she had to obliterate the place where her parents died. She never wanted to see this place again. She removed another black ball from her jacket, lobbed it onto the front porch and again screamed, *"Eradico!"*

Fire consumed the only home she'd ever had. She wished she could destroy her whole past so easily.

She jumped into the car and sped away.

CHAPTER SIX

Marietta, Ohio

CLAIRE SAT AT the dining room table eating yet another Lean Cuisine. She'd already taken a shower and tucked herself into Henry's high school football jersey. Her nightly routine was simple. Put on a nightie. Eat. Brush her teeth. Pick a book. Make tea. Go to bed.

Sitting on the table just inches from the plastic tray was her colorful friend. As she ate sesame chicken, she stared at the owl head. She put down her fork and turned the statue around. She wished she knew where to find Natasha. Maybe her old friend could shed some light on the unusual find.

Abandoning her dinner, she took the owl to the couch and sat down to study it. With the tip of her forefinger, she traced the owl's beak. Electricity jolted through her. The statue tumbled to the floor as she fell backward onto the couch.

Everything went dark.

Broken Heart, Oklahoma

ASH WOKE WITH the certain knowledge that someone was in the room. She whipped the blade from under her pillow and pressed it against the throat of the man hovering above her.

"Hello," croaked Jarod.

"Jesus H. Christ!" She removed the knife and rolled across the bed. She sat up and glared at him. "Do you have a death wish?"

"I wanted to check on you."

"Why?"

Jarod shook his head. "You don't like it when people care, do you?"

"Ugh. Spare me." Ash flopped back onto the bed. "How are the Huntsons?"

"You did good. Everyone is safe. Broken Heart will be the sanctuary Rick and his daughter needs. The little girl is special. She definitely belongs here."

Ash had sensed the same thing in Margaret.

"Yeah. I'm glad about that." After Ash had gotten to Broken Heart, Queen Patsy and a battalion of vampire mothers descended upon Rick and Margaret. They'd been washed, fed, hugged, and finally, put to bed in one of the rooms at the Three Sisters Bed and Breakfast. Ash had gotten a room, too, and immediately passed out.

She considered Jarod's declaration about letting people care about her. Ash cleared her throat. "Soul shifting takes a lot out of me."

Jarod made himself comfortable on the bed and opened his arms. "C'mere."

"What for?"

"To snuggle."

Ash grimaced. "Sounds weird."

"Natasha. Come here right now and snuggle with me."

"All right, all right. Just stop saying the word snuggle." Ash scooted across the bed and settled in Jarod's arms. He felt warm and cozy, a cocoon of tender strength she'd never had before. She felt herself relax. With her face pressed against his chest, she fell asleep.

ASH STOOD AT the entrance to the crypt. It was dark and raining. The cold drops clung to her lashes and rolled down her cheeks. She pushed on the metal gate barring the entrance and it swung open. She hurried inside and stopped. Lit candles in wall sconces offered dim light. And there, the altar was right where it should be.

Hands trembling, she brought the statue to the edge of the stone of platform. The figurine slipped. It tumbled to the stone floor and shattered.

Red smoke erupted and cruel feminine laughter filled the air. "You can't stop me," cried Lilith. "The world will burn, Ash. The world will burn."

ASH SHOT UP, the covers falling away. As the nightmare faded, she realized she was safe. And she wasn't alone.

"Natasha?"

Ash looked down at Jarod. His dark eyes were on her. "You okay?"

At some point, Jarod had discarded all his clothes but his boxers, and she was in a tank top and bootie shorts. Her gaze dropped to the hard-on tenting his silk boxers.

She lifted an eyebrow.

"Sleeping next to you has that effect."

Ash felt the hot pulse of lust, and she thought about leaning down and licking that delectable cock. She bit her lower lip. Rubbing her mouth over that velvet flesh, feeling it penetrate her throat, his hands in her hair, his groans of pleasure echoing in her ears … yes, please.

Ash couldn't keep her gaze off his erection. She couldn't quite stop herself from crawling between his legs and stripping off his underwear. She cupped his balls. One hand wrapped around his shaft and stroked it.

Jarod groaned, his eyes closing as she pleasured him.

Her lips descended, sliding down his flesh, sucking him deeply. Her body throbbed with primal heat. She felt so overwhelmed by the need to pleasure this man, she could barely breathe. His fingers slid into her hair as she licked and sucked his cock.

Ash loved his musky scent, the taste of his maleness. She didn't want to stop, and soon, she gained a rhythm that made him groan, made him beg for release. Ash stroked the base of his shaft as her mouth took him. The rhythm she created made him cry out, and before she understood what had happened, Jarod lifted her away and plastered her against the bed, rolling on top of her.

Ash's heart pounded as erotic heat poured through her. Her skin was so sensitized that the velvety fabric of the bedcovers brushing her naked thighs offered tiny thrills of pleasure. Her nipples hardened, her breasts filled with the ache to know Jarod's touch.

He lowered himself between her legs, and she gasped as he grazed the quivering flesh of her inner thighs.

She hadn't dated, much less taken a lover in God knew how many years. Any time she felt frisky, she took care of it herself. But this ... this was much better.

He shimmied off her shorts and tossed them off the bed. The press of his mouth against her panties, pushing so enticingly against her most feminine core made her moan.

Ash wanted more. She took off her shirt and wiggled off her panties.

"You're beautiful," said Jarod. "So beautiful, Natasha."

He nibbled on her hips and licked her belly. His tongue dipped into her navel. He slid lower still. His hands snaked around her thighs, and he pressed his mouth against her.

Delicious, sensual fire rolled over Ash, causing her to arch against his mouth. His wicked tongue darted in and out of her, the strokes rough and fast.

Bliss coiled tight and hot. Just as an orgasm threatened to overwhelm her, her lover pulled away.

"Damn it!" she cried.

Chuckling, he inserted two fingers inside her wet heat and started licking her clit again. The thrusts of his fingers matched those of his tongue. Her pleasure coiled tighter and tighter, but just as she might've gone over, he withdrew again.

"I'm gonna kill you."

"I'd prefer for you to love me."

His words electrified her as much as his hard body sliding oh-so-sensually against her.

His hands coasted over her stomach, drifting across her ribs, and then up to torment her breasts. Jarod paid her exquisite attention. His fingers found her nipples, rolled them into tight buds. He dragged his lips over her neck, the light rasp of his tongue tasting the spot under her ear. She shuddered and pressed her restless hands against his head, threading her fingers through his silky hair.

His tongue thrust into her mouth, and she could feel his desperation, his need. It matched her own. His fingers dipped through her curls to tease her swollen clit.

She stroked the muscled contours of his back. His tight buttocks flexed under her palms. Her hands wandered every inch of his muscled flesh as she pressed closer, moaning.

His cock nestled against her wet heat, nudging her entrance.

"Please," she murmured. "Please."

His cock inched inside her. Ash moaned, the velvety-smooth penetration stretching her wide.

When he was fully sheathed, she wrapped her legs around his waist and met his slow, measured thrusts.

The light hair on his chest abraded her nipples and caused sensation to ripple all the way to the heat building so deliciously between her thighs.

Ash felt the pleasure rise sharply. She panted, her nails digging into his ass. He didn't seem to mind.

"Oh God! Jarod!" She went over the edge, flying into sparkling bliss. As she rode the crest, she heard him groan. He stilled suddenly before his hips jerked against her and his harsh pants brushed against her neck as he spasmed inside her.

After the orgasm subsided, he rose on his elbows and gave Ash a tender kiss. "You are amazing."

She grinned, feeling exhausted but happy—a totally weird combination for her. "You're not so bad yourself.

Las Vegas, Nevada

AT THE SOUL searchers office, Nor stared at the headless lion. He could hardly believe a super powerful demon would use such a piece of crap as her vessel.

You couldn't account for some people's tastes.

With no computer, Nor relied on his smartphone to Google information about Lilith. After reading several articles, he concluded that was she was a horrible bitch. He'd texted with Ash last night. He knew that after she did a soul shift, she'd pass out for a good twelve hours.

God, he was bored.

He missed Ash's smartassery.

But he was thrilled with the appearance of Jarod the Gorgeous. He hoped his BFF let Jarod into her life. The man obviously cared about her, even if he'd resurrected the Convocation. Ash in love. Nor grinned. Bet his little soul shifter didn't see that coming.

The office felt stuffy, even in the early morning hours without the sun beating down on those stupid enough to live in a desert. Nor propped open the door with a banker's box filled with paperwork neither he nor Ash would file. They didn't enjoy the mundane tasks that came with operating a business, so they both ignored it all.

"I could probably absorb this information better if we could turn on the lights. And have the ability to make coffee." He rubbed his temples. "Oh, electricity how I miss you!"

The sudden, massive presence had Nor pushing out of his chair. His heart hammering, he looked everywhere. He couldn't see anyone, not even with his lycan vision. His stomach curdled as the smell of sulfur infiltrated the entire office.

Demon. Cold fear rushed over him. Intending to speed dial Ash, he grabbed his phone, but it was yanked from his grasp and thrown against the wall. The phone shattered.

The demon appeared. The creature was the size of Mack truck. His large eyes were red, and his bumpy skin was black. Rows of sharp teeth filled his evilly grinning mouth. "Give me the vessel."

Nor looked down at the lion body on the desk and grabbed it. He took off toward the break room, thinking maybe he could barricade it and then escape out the window. Going out the front was not an option. Nor burst through the door, but he barely got inside before the demon caught him. He scooped the lion out of Nor's grip and backed the shifter against the wall.

Nor growled and started shifting. Getting into his wolf form would up his chances of survival.

The demon laughed, and slapped a cold, scaly palm against the werewolf's neck. The shift instantly reversed, turning Nor into his more vulnerable human self. Burning pain seared his flesh, and he cried out. The demon got in his face and bared its teeth. "Tell Ash that Lilith says hello."

CHAPTER SEVEN

Broken Heart, Oklahoma

ASH SAT IN bed propped up on pillows while she scanned the news on her tablet. Jarod had gone downstairs to get breakfast for them both. She'd texted Nor, but hadn't heard back from him. The man took forever to get ready in the mornings, so she wasn't too concerned about his lack of response. Ash couldn't stop the smile when she thought about telling Nor she'd slept with Jarod.

More than that, actually.

She'd connected with him. It was a new feeling, and one she surprisingly enjoyed.

Someone knocked. Ash got up, slipped on Jared's shirt, which reached her knees, and answered the door.

"Rick."

"Hi, Natasha."

Ash winced. She hated the reminder of her painful past. The only time the name didn't raise the ugly memories was when Jarod used it. "Please call me Ash."

He nodded. "Ash. Sure. May I come in?"

She gestured for him to enter. After he walked inside, she shut the door. "How are you feeling?"

"Pretty awful really." He huffed out a breath. "You told Maggie that Sarah—my wife—was dead."

"She asked me, I told her."

"You don't tell a kid that her mom's dead."

"I do a lot of things, Rick, but I don't lie."

He swallowed hard and briefly closed his eyes. "So, she really is dead."

"Yes. I'm sorry," Ash said softly. "Do you remember what happened?"

"We were making dinner. Maggie had just finished her bath and was supposed to be picking up her toys. I smelled this … Jesus, I don't know … like something rotten. Something burning. Everything in the kitchen went wild. I heard this horrible laughter then the knives flew off the counter and…" He didn't finish, but he looked devastated. Waking to a life ruined was a feeling she knew all too well. "I can't believe this is happening."

The silence that stretched between them was filled with seven kinds of misery. She had spent so long shoving down her feelings, that a moment like this one felt like getting filleted by a dull knife. Jarod had cracked the walls around her heart. Now she was feeling shit hardcore. So much for my mind of steel and heart of stone.

She took his hand and squeezed. "Make a life here, Rick. You and Margaret are protected in Broken Heart."

"We don't have anywhere else to go." He glanced

at her. "Are sure Maggie is safe here?"

"Yes," said Ash simply.

"She's still asleep. She cried herself practically into a coma."

Ash's gut twisted. The kid had been so strong on the ride to Broken Heart. Her dad had been unconscious the whole trip, and she'd never once shed a tear. She'd waited until she'd felt safe—safe enough to grieve. Ash admired the little girl. Margaret and Rick had a shot at a real second chance in Broken Heart, but she knew that healing often hurt worse than the initial wound.

"Trust me when I say you both will survive. It won't feel that way for a long while, but day by day it gets better." The loss of her mother would either make Margaret stronger or break her completely. Ash bet on stronger. "I'm leaving this morning. Say good-bye to her for me."

"I will." He turned and then stopped, looking over his shoulder. "Thank you."

After he left, Ash flopped back onto the bed. Cripes. Caring about people was crazy hard work.

Marietta, Ohio

CLAIRE AWOKE SUDDENLY, her body soaked with sweat and her heart pounding. She sat up and snapped on the tiny lamp.

What the hell just happened?

Nightmares were nothing new. She often dreamed of the accident. And her dreams, terrifying or not, were always in color. Her last image of Henry was his bloodied face, his gaze filled with pain. Those horrors had faded, but watching the light go out of her fiancé's eyes was not a memory she would ever forget.

This nightmare had been different, though. It hadn't involved Henry. Instead, she'd ran through a cemetery, fear keeping a constant tempo with her heartbeat. The full moon glinted off a marble crypt, and she headed toward it. Relief filled her as she darted through the doorway.

The small building was empty. Candles in wall sconces offered dim light. Against the back wall was an altar. Incense sticks lodged around the top emitted thin trails of fragrant smoke from their burning ends. Two fat red candles sat on either side of an empty space.

The idol was missing.

"You can be with him again," a voice whispered on the wind whistling through the sarcophagus. "I can reunite you."

The air stilled. The candles flickered around the empty space. "You hold the key." The voice, distinctly female, grew stronger. "Do you love him enough? Are you brave enough to risk everything for Henry?"

Claire shuddered. She swung her legs off the bed and wiggled her toes against the shag carpet. It had all seemed so real. She couldn't begin to decipher all the symbols. Or was it ... literal? She nearly discarded the thought but hesitated. If she interpreted the nightmare literally, then she had some sort of object that would fit into that alcove. And the crypt existed.

Ever present grief speared her. The dream had presented her with an offer. A sacrifice that would reunite her with the only man she'd ever love. In a way, it was worse than seeing Henry's bloodied face. The dream had made her hope, and there was nothing more wounding in the stark face of waking reality. Tears crowded her eyes. She fell onto her side and wept into her pillow. When she couldn't cry anymore, she pried open her puffy, aching eyes.

The owl head, bright red and glowing in a sea of gray, stared at her from the nightstand.

Claire sat up and swept the owl into her shaking hands. This was the treasure. The only color she'd seen in a whole year. It had been in the living room when she'd gone to bed.

How had it ended up on her nightstand?

Had she really awoken from the nightmare? Maybe she was still in it. Or maybe she'd finally gone insane. She reached over and turned on the bedside lamp. Her gray world collapsed, and the whole room became vivid with colors. The sight left her confused and crazed.

Claire turned the owl around in her hands. She'd trade her own soul to see Henry one more time. Maybe she had gone insane, but she didn't care. A cheap, red owl head couldn't hurt her.

Claire felt the oppressive presence immediately. She gasped for air as icy fear coated her.

Before her appeared a massive creature that belonged only in nightmares.

This isn't real. I'm still dreaming.

The creature placed his scaly claws on her head. "You are the sacrifice that will free my queen, and you will be reunited with your love. Come, human. Thy destiny awaits."

Broken Heart, Oklahoma

AFTER BREAKFAST, ASH and Jarod left the

Three Sisters. Ash patted the pocket that protected the silver-painted clay snake. They'd been calling it a necklace, but it was more like a bracelet. It was just as cheap and gaudy looking as the lion's body.

"How do we find the third piece?" she asked.

"I think it will find us." He nodded at the couple walking toward them.

"Hi," said the dark-haired man. "I'm Matt Dennison, and this is my wife Natalie."

"Hi. I'm Ash. He's Jarod."

"Sorry to be abrupt," said Natalie, " but I have a very persistent spirit named Henry, who says his fiancé is in trouble."

"You're from the Amahté Family," said Jarod. The Amahté vampires could see and interact with ghosts and other types of spirits.

"Yes." Natalie grabbed Ash's hands. "Claire Glass lives in Marietta, Ohio. She's under the influence of a demon. He's taking her to some old cemetery there—one they don't even use anymore. You'll find her in a black marble crypt at the back edge of the property."

Shocked, Ash stared at the woman. "Claire Glass? Are you sure?"

Natalie looked off to the right and then nodded.

"She was my best friend from elementary through high school."

"Well, I guess this part will make sense to you then." Natalie's lips thinned. "Maybe. Henry says, Claire has the owl. She is the third sacrifice."

Matt took Natalie's hand and drew his wife into his embrace. "Good luck, Ash" he said.

"I'm sorry I can't tell you more," Natalie added. Together, they turned and walked away.

Adrenaline spiked in Ash's belly. Fear beat a

mantra in her mind: Hurry, hurry, hurry.

"Let's get to the cemetery," said Ash. "We have to get to Claire before the demon kills her."

"We need the lion and the snake," Jarod said.

"Are you sure that's a good idea?" Ash knew what the prophecy said, but it was a huge risk to have all three pieces together.

"It's the only way to truly stop her. She already has the first two sacrifices, if she manages to make your friend the third, the only hope we have is to trap her in the statue."

"Okay," Ash agreed. She didn't like the plan, but a bad plan at this point was better than no plan. Besides, Claire's life and the fate of the world left her little choice. "Let's go."

CHAPTER EIGHT

Marietta, Ohio

CLAIRE DIDN'T DRIVE anymore. Color was an intrinsic part of most traffic signs. And not being able to see red or green at stoplights was problematic. To go anywhere, she had to take the bus. Her mind felt clouded. Every so often, she'd surface from the fog and wonder what was happening. The demon, hiding in human form, would smile at her, look deeply into her eyes, and she'd fall into fog once more.

The nearest stop to the cemetery was six blocks away. With the demon holding her hand, they got off the bus. Cold rain drizzled. The chilly drops pelted her face and dribbled down her neck.

They hurried along the sidewalk. The glare from the streetlights highlighted the graffiti-filled walls, the trash-strewn gutter, and the barred windows of the closed businesses. Most were pawnshops interspersed with a beauty shop, a gun store, and a Mexican restaurant with filmy windows.

The man wore Henry's clothes, and Claire felt a burble of guilt. She shouldn't have kept any of his clothes. It wasn't like he would ever be able to wear them again. Seeing Henry's button-down shirt and crisp khakis on the demon made her angry, but the emotion was a dull throb. She couldn't figure out how to change what was happening.

"Not far now," he said, his toothy smile flashing at her, sharp and white.

Claire trudged beside him, unable to protest.

The red owl sat in her purse. Waiting.

Las Vegas, Nevada

AFTER THEY ARRIVED at Soul Searchers via the exploded atom method of travel, Ash yelled, "Nor! We need the lion."

She paused. Something felt wrong. The hair stood up on the back of her neck. "Nor?"

"Why is it so hot in here?" asked Jarod. "Don't you use the air conditioner?"

"It requires electricity."

"You don't have electricity?" Jarod's dark eyebrows winged upward. He pulled a cell phone out of his front pocket and hit a single number. "I'm at the office of Soul Searchers, just off Fremont in Las Vegas. Get us electricity. Take care of every debt and bill related to this office, to Natasha Nelson, and to Sedrick North. Just start a running account."

Within a few minutes, the lights flickered on. Her

computer re-booted. The rest of the office machines beeped to electronic life. Best of all, cold air began to pour into the room. Ash wasn't sure if she should be pissed off or grateful. She went for a combo. "Thanks, but you don't have to fix my problems."

"Did I mention that I'm filthy rich?" asked Jarod.

"Oh." Ash smiled. "Nor will really want to keep you now for being both filthy and rich."

"As long as you do, too."

Ash felt herself blush. Blush, for God's sake. She walked around Jarod so he wouldn't see her reddened face.

Ash strode across the room and opened the door to the tiny kitchen with its single table and two chairs. "Nor!" Her partner lay on the floor. If she didn't know better, she'd think he had passed out from one of his typical booze 'n love fests, but his body was too still, his face overly pale. She squatted next to him, panic rising within her.

"Nor? Nor!" Ash patted his cheeks, afraid to check for a pulse.

Jarod knelt next to her. "What's that on his neck?"

She peered at the three slanted lines enclosed in a circle. Nor didn't have any tattoos. How the hell had this one gotten on him? "I don't know."

Jarod pressed his fingertips against Nor's carotid artery. "He's alive."

Relief cascaded through Ash. "We need a healer."

"I agree." Jarod retrieved his phone and pushed a button. "Patrick, is your Mom around? Ask her to come to Soul Searchers—yes, Natasha's office in Vegas. We have an emergency."

Two seconds after Jarod's call, a red-haired goddess dressed in a diaphanous green gown arrived in a shower of gold sparks.

"Brigid," said Jarod. "Thank you for coming."

She knelt down and examined the prone werewolf. "Demon poison. I haven't seen that symbol in a while." Her sharp gaze sliced Ash. "The sign of Lilith."

"Shit." Ash was officially pissed. And she was going to kill Lilith. "This is my lycan, Brigid. Mine. Do not let him die."

"I will do all in my power to keep him alive." Brigid picked up the six foot four, 240-pound man as if he weighed no more than a bag of feathers. "If you don't stop Lilith, I can only postpone the inevitable. If she is able to manifest, her power will be too strong for me to abate. Your friend will become one of her minions."

Ash understood all too well what Brigid implied. If she didn't stop Lilith, Nor would be lost to her. The lycan wouldn't want a life without choices, certainly not a life ruled by an evil puppet master. "Brigid...If we can't stop her...Nor. He wouldn't want..." Ash choked down the emotion welling inside her. "He hates to wear black."

"I understand, Ash." Brigid smiled. "I'll take him to Broken Heart. Come when you can." She and Nor sparkled out of sight.

Heart pounding, Ash strode to her desk, pulled open a file drawer and grabbed the box that held the lion's body. She tore off the lid and swore.

It was empty.

"Fucking demons." She tossed the box to the floor and kicked the desk, furious. She'd sent Nor home with the statue. She'd put him in danger. It was her fault. Her parents. Rick's wife. Claire. And now Nor.

"Fucking bitch!" she screamed, tears running in hot streaks down her cheeks .

Jarod wrapped her in his arms and stroked her hair as he held her against his chest. "We'll stop them at the cemetery, Natasha. Lilith won't win."

For a moment, she took his comfort, but she knew she had to get her emotions under control. She stepped out of Jarod's embrace and nodded sharply. Her jaw clenched with her barely contained fury. She would teach Lilith just who was the biggest, baddest bitch in the land. The demon queen would regret challenging Ash.

"Let's go."

Jarod took her hand, and in seconds, they were gone, cells exploding and zipping along, on a direct path to Lilith.

Marietta, Ohio

IN THE AWFUL crypt, Claire fought the hold the demon had on her. She surfaced from the mind-fog and backed away, clutching her purse. That owl head was the key to this whole mess. She knew that she couldn't let him have it, not for anything.

He put a headless lion into the candle-lit alcove. "Place the owl head on the lion's body!"

"Why?" she whispered.

"It does not matter. Do as I say!" He lifted his arm as though he meant to strike her. She hunkered against the wall, and screamed.

THE RUSTED IRON GATE sported a damaged sign: Garden Hill Cemetery. The narrow road that led into the defunct cemetery was several feet to the left of the crumbling mortuary. The gate opened easily, so it wasn't exactly high security.

Sheeting rain pelted them, but Ash shrugged off the storm. She understood the dark. She thrived in it. But this wasn't about her survival, it was about her friends. Nor and Claire first, she thought, then the world. She didn't want to think about how her drag queen werewolf was fighting for his life, or how her childhood friend might lose hers.

Jarod took her hand and squeezed. With that simple gesture he reminded Ash that for once, she wouldn't be alone. Not ever.

"Thank you," she said.

"For what?"

She lifted his hand, their fingers twining together, fitting perfectly as if born in union. "For finding me."

"You're my other half. My mate," Jarod said. "I'll always find you."

Ash nodded, then let him go. They'd need their hands free for the upcoming fight, but that little bit of contact had bolstered her will and strengthened her resolve. "Okay. Let's go kick some demon ass."

Together, they strode through cracked and crumbling gravestones. Within minutes, they saw the black marble crypt on a small hill.

Ash cataloged her assets. Knives. Sig. Therianthrope. Tonight, she wore white jeans and a white T-shirt, which looked pretty good with her pink leather jacket. Nor was forever trying to get her to wear more colors, but he always went for out-there shades that made her flinch. Her heart squeezed. She wanted to see him with her own eyes—just to know he really was okay. She patted a zipped pocked on the inside of her jacket. It hid the snake necklace. The final piece of the puzzle.

Please, don't let me be too late.

The black marble crypt was small—maybe ten feet wide and nearly as tall. They were approaching from the south side, so they couldn't really see the front of it. The closer they got, the slower and quieter they became.

Two flashes of sparkling gold appeared to their left. She had her gun whipped out and aimed at the same time Jarod pointed his staff, crackling magic at the ready.

Lorcan and Patrick stood there, looking fearsome, especially with their fangs exposed. "We hear some demons need ass kickin'," said Patrick.

"You heard right." Ash was glad for the back-up. Especially from two of the most powerful parakind in Broken Heart. The twins were the sons of the first vampire ever made, Ruadan. And Lorcan had werewolf in him as well.

While, she hated being without Nor, she couldn't have asked for two better men, along with Jarod, to back her up in this fight. Still, she missed Nor. She always felt better going into a hinky situation with him at her side. The man could throw a punch like Mike Tyson and pin bad guys with a well-placed stiletto. But Lilith wasn't your average bad guy, and she'd already taken out Nor without lifting a finger.

The four of them hurried as a unit toward the slight incline. Just as they reached the south wall, the rain returned with a vengeance. Ash was soaked in seconds, but it didn't matter. Her mind was focused on their goal. She scuttled along the wall, turned the corner, and slipped toward the doorway. She stopped at the edge of the entrance and peeked around it.

Candles offered dim light in the dark space. She saw the demon immediately. He was nearly seven feet tall, his obsidian skin as bumpy as a toad's. His eyes glowed an awful red.

Ash's heart jumped into her throat. She knew instinctively that was the creature who'd tried to kill her in that Las Vegas alleyway. Jarod gripped her shoulder. His touch, like magic, shed the terror from her like molting skin. She could see the demon for what he really was, another evil fuck-twit to vanquish from this plane of existence. She'd let fear cripple her for a moment, a testament to the demon queen's power and reach.

But no more. It was time to focus on the task at hand.

Kicking Lilith's ass.

Ash's gaze shifted to the thin, trembling woman. Claire. An older version of the girl she once knew. Her old friend looked drained, her expression confused, her eyes glazed.

Ash scooted back and leaned toward the men. "Surprising that asshole is our only advantage."

"We'll take the demon," said Jarod.

Relieved, she nodded. "I'll get Claire and destroy the complete vessel." She'd have to put the pieces together then destroy it before Lilith managed to kill Claire and use the statuary as a conduit to this world.

She slipped out a dagger from her left boot and then hurried into the crypt with Jarod and the two vampires right behind her.

CHAPTER NINE

WHEN THEY ENTERED the sanctum, Claire looked at them, her eyes wide and glazed. She huddled in the corner hugging her purse, her thin body quaking as tears tracked her cheeks. Pure fear lit her gaze.

Jarod, Patrick, and Lorcan headed toward the demon. Ash bee-lined to Claire. She bent down. "Claire? It's Natasha. I'm here to help you." She gestured to the altar that housed the lion's body. "Do you have the owl?"

Claire nodded. Her fingers were embedded in the purse, and Ash wasn't sure if she could pry it out of the woman's hands.

"He tricked me," she whispered.

"I know." Ash sheathed her knives then slipped her hands under the purse and tugged it. "C'mon, honey. Let go."

Claire's fingers unclenched. Ash took the freed bag, unzipped it, and pawed through the contents. She found the owl head and pulled it out. Claire moaned in terror, covering her eyes with her hands. Ash put the purse next to Claire and patted her hand. The woman was in no condition to escape on her own. In fact, her breathing was too shallow and she was overly pale. "Hang on," said Ash. "Just hang on."

Ash dropped the bright red owl head on the marble floor. It instantly shattered. She grabbed the lion from the alcove and threw it hard, relishing the sound of its destruction. She withdrew the snake from her pocket and dropped it, stepping on it with her boot heel. Obliterating Lilith's vessel wasn't enough. Not for all the pain the demon had caused. Ash stomped the bits into dust.

Triumphantly, she turned toward Lilith's demon flunky. It had fallen to its knees. Patrick and Lorcan held on to the monster's arms, but it appeared to take some effort to keep him immobile. Jarod stood over him, silver balls of magic pulsed above his palms. The demon bared its teeth and growl. "I am the doorway for Lilith!"

"Sorry, buddy," said Ash. "The door's closed."

The demon's laughter echoed into the room. "My queen is more clever than you." His red-eyed gaze dropped to the destroyed statue, and his toothy grin widened.

"What's he talkin' about?" asked Patrick.

Ash didn't like that the demon was so unconcerned about the destruction of the statue. What else was there left to do?

"Natasha!" The alarm in Jarod's voice had her

looking at the ground.

The snake had not been destroyed.

It had come alive.

It wiggled up Ash's body with supernatural speed. She grabbed at it, but it was like trying to capture smoke.

Jarod released his magic and rushed to his mate. He, too, tried to capture the little beast. "Fuck!"

The snake wrapped around her wrist. It pulsed hotly, glowing like a burning ember and started sinking into her skin.

"It's you!" the demon shouted with glee. "It was you all along."

Ash cried out as she attempted to break the snake's hold on her wrist. Even with Jarod helping, the totem would not budge.

Jarod whirled toward the demon. "What have you done to her?"

"*She* is the vessel, fool," cackled the demon. "Lilith will live in her and Ash the Destroyer will be no more."

The snake embedded into Ash's muscle. Spikes of pain caused her to cry out, and she regretted that small show of weakness.

"By your own hand the last sacrifice will be made, Ash the Destroyer, and in that act, you shall be destroyed. From your ashes, my queen shall be reborn."

Hatred stabbed Ash with poisoned blades, but she couldn't stop herself from raising the dagger clenched in her fist. She held it over the shaking body of her friend.

No! Not Claire. Not anybody. She thought of Nor, his life in her hands. And Jarod. He was her mate.

She'd finally found love, and now, with a demon controlling her will, she would lose everything.

Pain radiated down her arm and throbbed in her shoulder, up her neck, right into her jaw.

"Natasha," Claire said, her voice heavy. Her eyes closed. She whispered, "Where's Henry?"

The darkness slithered inside Ash, and she knew it was only a fraction of the horror Lilith would unleash.

Ash used every ounce of her will to keep from plunging the blade into her friend's heart. A difficult feat when everything inside her screamed to *kill the sacrifice*.

Ash struggled to regain control. She focused completely on her hand and arm, forcing her straining muscles away from Claire. It took a herculean effort to place the poisoned dagger against her own throat.

Time to end Lilith once and for all.

CHAPTER TEN

"NO!" JAROD GRABBED her wrist, but not even his animal strength could wrest the blade from her grip. "I won't lose you."

"It's the only way," Ash huffed. "If she completely possesses me, it'll be over. For everyone."

"Then fight, damn it." He held on tightly. "Use my energy, my strength. You can defeat her."

Ash took shuddering breaths. She accepted the power Jarod gave her, flowing silver light that fortified her, calmed her.

Inhaling a deep breath, Ash closed her eyes and delved into her psychic core. The hundreds of souls she'd consumed over the years appeared as long strands of pulsating color that twirled around, an endless rainbow of essences. Lilith's slimy evil darkness swirled among those colors, a tattered black ribbon that oozed poison.

Ash wasn't sure what to do. How was she supposed to fight a demon? True demons had no souls. Lilith could eat the ones here like Skittles to gain power and strength.

No. Ash had to conquer Lilith from within. She hadn't sacrificed Claire, so Lilith's hold wasn't finite. She psychically reached for the black ribbon, shuddering as liquid hate soaked her.

Lilith's essence clung to her like thick grease, and Ash found it difficult to get purchase. While she slipped and faltered, Lilith clung more tightly, digging spiky tendrils into Ash's very heart. *Kill Claire. Kill Claire. Kill Claire.* The impulse felt insurmountable.

"Get her out of here," Ash screamed, hoping someone, anyone would take Claire from her sight. She couldn't fight Lilith while she fought the urge to murder her friend.

You can do this, Natasha, a different voice said. Jarod's voice. *Fight, babe. Fight.*

She'd heard of mate bonds giving couple the ability to communicate through telepathy, and Jarod's voice loving voice helped her drown out the homicidal one. Emboldened by Jarod's courage, she grabbed onto Lilith's ugly presence.

For a moment, Ash felt the demon's rage, the sociopathic urges to destroy everything within reach returned. She was heartless. Soulless. Chaotic energy with only one purpose: Annihilate. Ash might be the destroyer of souls, but Lilith was the destroyer of worlds.

Jarod's magic bolstered her again. She focused on escaping the demon queen's hold on her will. Silver joined her white and blue magic, and like pythons they surrounded Lilith's essence and squeezed.

The blade fell from Ash's fierce grip as the demon raged and struggled. She held on tightly, Jarod working as one with her, until they'd completely smote the evil that had been named Lilith.

The inky blackness inside her exploded.

Searing pain slashed through Ash, ripping a scream from throat.

Ash fell to her knees, and Jarod was there, to hold her up.

Two beams of silvery-blue light shot out from Ash's eyes, and encompassed Lilith's demon henchman. Patrick and Lorcan wisely let go and stepped away, backing as far into the shadows as they could.

The demon screamed like a feral animal, unable to break free of Ash and Jarod's combined magic.

The creature glared at her, his red eyes dimming as his life was drained. His body twitched. Black blood dribbled from his nose and mouth.

His eyes went glassy, and his body convulsed one last time.

Ash collapsed and Jarod caught her.

"Natasha?"

She inhaled a shaky breath. "I feel like Nor tap-danced on me in spiked heels."

Jarod laughed, and kissed her. Ash had never felt so drained or exhausted.

Or loved.

"What happened to Lilith?" asked Lorcan.

"She's gone."

"Back t' hell then?" Patrick's silver gaze pinned hers.

"No," said Ash. "She is no more."

"That's impossible," Lorcan said. "Demons can't be killed."

"They can now." When Jarod's power had intertwined with her own, much as their fingers had, she'd been able to do what had, in the past, been an impossibility.

At that moment, as if to add emphasis to her new ability, the creature's corpse dissolved into sulfuric black powder.

"How's Claire?" she asked in a hoarse voice. She knew she'd pass out any minute, and probably sleep for a week.

Patrick and Lorcan checked on the human woman. "I'm sorry, Ash," said Patrick softly. "She's dead."

"How?" Ash hadn't killed her friend like Lilith wanted, so how had Claire died?

Lorcan placed his hand on the woman's chest. "The demon weakened her too much. I think her heart just gave out."

"She wanted to see Henry," said Ash. She said a silent good-bye to her old friend. "I hope he's waiting for her.

Ash leaned on Jarod, allowing him to take her weight. Her burden. "Please take care of her," she whispered. She looked at Jarod, at the love and compassion shining in his eyes. "I'm gonna pass out now."

And she did.

CHAPTER ELEVEN

Somewhere on the other side...

CLAIRE AWOKE IN a daze. The first thing she noticed was that she could see color. The glory of the green-leafed trees pitched against the cloudless blue sky dazzled her. Somehow, she'd gone from that dismal crypt to sitting on a wooden bench wearing her favorite yellow sundress and strappy sandals.

"Claire?"

She turned and saw Henry walking toward her. Behind him, she saw a well-worn path that led to the gleaming city in the distance.

With a cry of happiness, she leapt from the bench and threw herself into his arms. He hugged her tightly, and she wept, so thrilled to feel his embrace.

"Am I dreaming?" she asked.

"You died, Claire. You're in the next world. I've been waiting for you."

She took a moment to consider his words, and realized he spoke the truth. Relief was so palpable she could almost taste it. "How is this possible?"

"I had a little help from some friends."

"Natasha?"

"Yes, and some other nice folks from a town called Broken Heart."

She stared at the love of her life, memorizing every feature of his face from his chiseled jaw, the slight bump in his nose, the little scar that marked the left side of his chin, as if at any moment he'd suddenly be taken away again. "I missed you," she said.

"I'm not going anywhere. This is our final destination, babe," he said. "This is forever."

"I couldn't take it if I lost you again."

"I have never left you, and I never will."

Relief and unabashed happiness lightened Claire's heart. "I love you, Henry."

"And I you," said Henry, his blue eyes twinkling and his familiar grin reassuring. He took her hand, and together they walked into eternity.

CHAPTER TWELVE

Broken Heart, Oklahoma

"NO. FUCKING. WAY." Nor examined the pair of sassy silver heels. "Ferragamos. In my size." He looked in the second shoebox and squealed. "Jimmy Choo. And pink! Oh, honey, what did you do? Hold up an Orange County housewife at knife point?"

"I'm dating a billionaire," said Ash.

Jarod put his arm around Ash and gave her smacking kiss. "She's totally in love with me."

Ash couldn't stop the blush. "I barely like you."

Jarod dipped his head down toward her ear. "Liar."

She blushed harder.

"Oh. Em. Gee. Ash getting embarrassed?" Nor pretended to wipe away an imaginary tear. "Our little soul shifter is all grown up."

"Ha, ha." Ash pointed to the shoes. "Keep it up and I'll return those."

"Over my dead body." Nor sat up, his plumped pillows falling to the wayside. His Highness was shored up in a king-sized bed, waited on hand and foot. Even though he looked a helluva lot better than he had a week ago, he was still too pale. After Lilith was destroyed, Brigid had managed to break the demon curse and save him, but Nor wasn't quite fully healed.

"So when's the wedding?" asked Nor, his expression innocent.

"We're leaving." Ash grabbed Jarod by the arm and jerked him toward the door.

"I want to be maid of honor," called out Nor. "I expect Prada, Jarod. Prada!"

Ash yanked Jarod out into the hallway of the Three Sisters Bed and Breakfast. She shut the door and blew out a relieved breath.

Jarod spun her around and took her into his arms. "Tell me you love me."

"You love me."

"Natasha…"

"Okay," she said. She grabbed his face and pulled him down to hers. "I love you."

She kissed him, putting her heart, and yes, her very own soul, into it. She pulled back, grinning like an idiot, and said, "I want my wedding dress to be made out of white leather."

"Whatever you want, my love," said Jarod. "Whatever you need."

"You," she said. "Just you."

BONUS MATERIAL #1
The Origin of Ash the Destroyer

SIXTEEN-YEAR-OLD Natasha Nelson paused at the backyard gate. At nearly one in the morning, nothing stirred, not even her dog, Jack. Her hand rested on the latch as she listened for the terrier. If he barked, he might wake Mom and Dad.

The sweet scent of honeysuckle wafted from the vines entwining the metal fence. She leaned down and tugged off a yellow blossom. Gently she pinched the stamen and withdrew it, licking away the pearl of nectar on its end.

Her mother had taught her how to do that.

Guilt crimped her stomach. She looked at the desecrated flower and wished she hadn't plucked it, hadn't stolen its honey. The yellow petals were already browning and curling inward. Sighing, she tossed it to the ground.

She unlatched the gate. As she pushed it open, the hinges squealed loudly. Crap! She stepped inside the backyard. Heart pounding, she stood still and listened for the rumbling yell of her father or the tapping of her mother's slippered foot on the back porch.

Wait a minute. When she'd crept out of her bedroom window a few hours ago, the front and back porch lights had been on. She hadn't even noticed the lack of illumination until now, a sure sign of her guilt. Or maybe it was that she'd always been able to see well in the dark. Her dad teased her about this quirk, calling her "cat eyes." It didn't help that her eye color hovered between gray and blue.

She pressed a palm against her warbling belly and studied the shadowy exterior of the house. It was a simple, one-story, three-bedroom house. It looked liked the others in the neighborhood. Normal. Plain. Boring.

Her gaze drifted away from the house and up to the sky. The full moon stared at her like the round eye of God. She felt that awful judgment of a deity she didn't know. Her parents were scientists, pragmatic to their very cores. They said that religion was for the superstitious and the weak-minded. But secretly, she believed that there was something, maybe someone, all-knowing and intelligent watching over the Earth. Watching over her. Judging her.

Sighing deeply, she trudged toward her bedroom window. Her room was in the back, just off the kitchen. Her parents slept in the bedroom in front of the house. Nerves jumping, she put her hand on the windowsill. The curtain blocked her view.

Oh, c'mon. If her parents weren't such stick-in-the-mud jerks, she wouldn't have had to sneak out to go to Rick's party.

Her face warmed. Rick Huntson was so nice. He had the bluest eyes and the cutest dimpled chin.

Tonight, he'd almost kissed her. Just remembering the close call in the kitchen, when he'd gotten her the second beer and leaned toward her, his eyes dipping to her mouth, made her feel all tingly and wonderful.

But his lips hadn't brushed hers. Instead, he said that he liked her T-shirt, which was blue and said "Baby Doll" in a glittery scroll across her chest. Her jean shorts were faded and tight. She'd given herself a pedicure—her toenails were sparkly blue—and wore black flip-flops.

Now, she felt unprotected in the summer clothing, as if she needed armor and shield to face what lay ahead. Even though it was nearly May, the air felt chilly. Her flesh goosepimpled and she rubbed her bare arms.

The window slid open easily. Tashie pushed aside the curtain and peered inside. She saw the familiar shapes of her bedroom: the twin bed with its fake occupant; the desk with its pile of books and papers; the listing floor lamp; and the boom box pushed against the closet door.

Nothing looked disturbed. Grinning with relief, she climbed inside and shut the window. She tossed off her flip-flops and thought about how to retrieve Jack. She wanted the companionship tonight. He was probably tucked into her parent's room, snoring away.

Quickly, she went into her private bathroom and rubbed off her make-up then she put on her pajamas. At least if her parents woke-up, she'd look as if she'd been tucked into bed all night.

When she opened her bedroom door and stepped into the kitchen, her skin prickled. The house was eerily quiet and too dark.

Something felt ... wrong.

Think it through, Tashie. Fear can always be displaced by logic. Remembering her father's advice steadied her. She tiptoed to the light switch and flicked it. The florescent bulbs kicked on and she looked around the kitchen. The normalcy of its yellow wallpaper and neat counters settled her.

She walked through the dining room and into the hallway. To the right was her Mom's office. Her Dad's lab equipment and other geekoid stuff took up most of the basement. She veered left then, as quietly as she could, Tashie turned the handle and opened the door.

Blech. It smelled terrible.

Her eyes roved over the inner darkness.

She saw the prone forms of her parents in their beds, and there, stretched between them, slept Jack. For a long moment, she stared.

"Mom? Dad?"

Her parents didn't stir.

Her heart pounded crazily as she flipped on the lights. Neither her mother nor father jolted up and admonished her for waking them.

She hurried to the bed, drew back the covers.

Blood. On them, on the bed, on Tashie's hands. She screamed and backed away, trying to process the horror. No, no, it wasn't true. Her eyes were playing tricks on her.

"J-jack?" She stumbled forward and reached out. She wanted to grab him, wanted to drag him away from the carnage, but he felt wrong. Like a toy that had lost its stuffing.

He was dead, too.

Someone had killed her dog. Someone had killed her parents. She fell to her knees and emptied her stomach, the fermented smell of vomit mixing with that awful rusted scent of blood.

She greedily sucked in oxygen as tears squeezed from her eyes. Bile rose in her throat and she tasted yeasty-sour beer. For a second, she thought she would puke again.

"Natasha."

She rolled onto her side and stared up at the thin creature with its round head and stick-like limbs. His eyes were red, his skin green, and his clothes tattered. He smelled like mold. He looked like death.

Her death.

"You were not here," he said in an incredibly beautiful voice—an angel's voice that did not match his devil's body. "So, I had a snack. Your mother tasted especially delicious—as I imagine you will taste."

"Get away from me!" She tried to kick at him, but he merely laughed. He bent down and grabbed her by the throat, lifting her easily, as if she weighed nothing. She flailed, trying to strike him with hands and feet.

"You will give me great power, my beautiful girl. With your blood, I will no longer live in the shadows. I will be revered. Feared."

He was crazy.

He was a psycho serial killer.

He was strong.

With his hand squeezing the breath out of her, she couldn't scream. Her limbs grew too heavy to move.

"Look at me, sweet Natasha."

She lifted her eyes to his monster gaze. Her stomach cramped so painfully, she opened her mouth to cry out. Only a rasp escaped. The pain throbbed through her unmercifully. Every nerve ending felt on fire.

And still she could not break the stare of the creature holding her.

I'm dying. He's killing me.

The pain welded her to the man. She felt … connected. Now, she could feel his shock, the coldness of his flesh, the fetid breath his wizened lungs, the double beats of two hearts.

Blue light erupted from her skin. Tendrils elongated and stretched, wrapping around him.

"No!" he shouted. "No!"

Tashie felt as though she had shouted the words. She was fused to him. His evil tasted as horrid as the bile crowding her throat.

The blue light glowed brighter and brighter. Through her terror and her graying vision, Tashie saw a strange, red radiance pulsing like a heartbeat. The small luminous globe radiated in the center of his being. It was so pretty. So warm. So alive.

She reached for it. Not with her arms, but with her mind. She plucked it from him, as if she were merely pulling off a ripe apple from an old tree.

He released her. She collapsed to the floor, inhaling in shaky breaths. She felt electrified.

Her gaze landed on the heap lying a foot away.

Tashie crawled to where the monster had fallen. She gripped a shoe and yanked, but there was no need. It was no longer attached to anything.

The murderer was gone.

WHEN TASHIE AWOKE, she found herself in a room she didn't recognize. Everything was white—the walls, the floor, the bed, the covers. Even though there were no beeping machines or IVs hooked up to her arm, she realized she must be in a hospital.

She felt sick, both hot and cold, and she shivered so hard her teeth chattered. A light blanket covered her and she simultaneously wanted to kick it off and draw it up to her chin.

A gentle hand pressed against her sweaty brow.

"Mom?"

The woman who knelt beside the bed was not her mother. She was dressed in a white robe, like the one Gandalf wore in that Lord of the Rings movie. Around her neck was a thick gold chain. Dangling from it was a glittering symbol: Two snakes winding through a heart pierced with a sword. What was she? A nun? A nurse? A professor at Hogwart's?

"I don't feel good." Tashie could barely get the words out. Her throat was so dry she felt as though she'd swallowed cotton.

"I know, Natasha. But your suffering will soon pass."

Tashie believed the woman. Her soothing voice was filled with confidence and sympathy.

"My name is Gwendolyn." The woman looked ageless. She wasn't young, wasn't old. She wore no make-up and her shiny brown hair was tucked into one long braid. Her brown eyes were filled with concern. Whoever she was, this mystery lady, she seemed truly worried about Tashie.

"Where are my mom and dad?"

"They're dead."

The unflinching confirmation of her worst nightmare brought all the memories flooding back. Mom and Dad sprawled in the bloodied bed. Jack's lifeless body. The creature so intent on killing her. Only she had somehow killed him. Hot tears fell and the sorrowful cry like that of a wounded animal escaped.

"No," she cried. It wasn't true. She had dreamed everything, the way she was dreaming now. *Wake up, Tashie. Wake up!* "No."

"Yes, Natasha. The sooner you deal with it, the sooner you can heal." Her no-nonsense tone was not unkind.

Tashie's mind, her body, her entire being rebelled against the idea of Mom and Dad being dead. How could she live in a world without her parents?

I hate you. I hate you. I hate you.

Those were the last words she had uttered to them. Oh, God.

Tashie leaned over the edge of the bed and vomited.

BONUS MATERIAL #2
Deleted Scene with Deleted Character

"**I'M SO NOT** in the mood to kill you."

"Terrific," said the same Irish voice of a female. "I'm not in the mood to die."

Sighing, Ash turned and looked down at the tiny woman standing next to her. The top of her head barely reached Ash's hip. She had a ton of red, curly hair, creamy skin, and eyes as green as summer grass. She wore Converse sneakers, faded jeans, and a T-shirt touting 'Van Halen Rules.'

"What are you? A midget?"

"If'n I was, I surely wouldn't like your terminology. Don't you know that humans with dwarfism like to be called 'little people'?"

Being politically correct was the least of Ash's worries. "You're not human."

"Thank Brigid for that! I'm a fairy, thank you very much."

Terrific. Ash unlocked the door and swung it open. "Go away. "Ash went into the hotel room. She flicked on the light, which cast a dim, yellow glow from the single bulb dangling from the ceiling.

The room didn't boast any amenities. Hell, not even the antiquated television sitting on the dresser worked. The twin beds were hard as rocks. The chair in the corner had stuffing popping out of several tears.

"Is this where you live then?"

"Nope," said Ash, staring at Jak.

"You lived in this city once, did you not?"

"Why do you care?"

The fairy shrugged, obviously not offended by Ash's curt behavior. She perched on the edge of the ugly chair.

Ash took off her jacket and tossed it onto the bed.

Jak examined her black, skin-tight pants tucked into sturdy black boots and her pink tank top. Hey, she might kick ass for a living, but she was still a girl.

"I recognize Bernie's work. Not many people get to wear his creations." Her gaze flicked to the jacket. "Did he make that, too?"

Ash shrugged. Jak had a keen eye. Her friend and literal fashion wizard Bernie made all of Ash's clothes. He knew how to make magical materials that wouldn't cut, burn, tear, or restrict. The jacket was one-of-a-kind. It had a dozen pockets. She could hide anything, huge or tiny, in them. They all offered endless storage, and the cloth stretched to accommodate just about any object.

Ash sat on the corner of the bed. "What do you want?"

Jak's gaze flitted around the terrible room as she picked at a thread on her jeans. The woman's nervousness was so great that it filtered through Ash's psychic shields. Jak played a good game, but nobody who liked living was completely unafraid of Ash. It was one thing to die. It was quite another to have your essence stolen and stored inside a being with the ability to assume your form. For creatures unfortunate enough to be absorbed by Ash, there was no afterlife. "Have you ever taken the soul of a fairy?"

"Yes." Ash felt a flicker of guilt, but she got over it. Most people born on the Earth got to choose what kind of lives they had. They went to school or traveled or took jobs and raised families. They worried about things like love and happiness and loss and sorrow. But for those few who were like Ash, there was never a choice. Sometimes, you were born into your destiny.

She couldn't change the fact that she was a soul shifter. But she had finally realized she could change who she worked for and how she lived the rest of her life. She would never have a family or a husband or a nine-to-five job. She would never be normal, never be anything other than what she'd been born. But how she used her gift was her choice, and hers alone.

Jak pursed her lips. "I like to think that you took those who needed taken. That maybe the Convocation's mission to keep the balance meant that you prevailed over evil." Her gaze met Ash's. "But that's probably not true, is it? If'n it was, why leave the service of those watching over the magic in this world?"

"What does it matter? The Convocation doesn't exist anymore," Ash lied. She was all too aware of their existence since Jarod's introduction. Frankly, she wasn't in the mood to play conversational Ping-Pong. Working for the Convocation meant maintaining the balance both ways. It wasn't very often that Ash had been sent to take down beings on the side of good. But whoever the Convocation marked, she'd taken down—good or bad.

"There are those among us that would like to see you dead."

"I'm aware."

The door flew open. Nor posed in the doorway, holding a paper bag in one arm and a bag of ice in the other. "I'm ba-ack!" He looked at the fairy and grinned, obviously delighted. "Yay! We have company. Drink?"

"None for me, thanks," said Jak.

Ash held up two fingers. "I'll have a double."

Nor strode to the dresser and unpacked everything needed to make a decent drink.

Jak watched Ash as if she could determine what kind of thoughts bounced around in her head. The fairy nodded, as if she'd made a decision. "I'm offering my services to you, Ash the Destroyer."

"I don't want your services."

"Now, wait a minute." Nor turned and handed a red cup to Ash. "It's a triple." Nor took his drink and sat next to Ash. "What kind of services? Spa? Massage? Barista?"

"I'm a healer. I know the ways of fixing spirit, body, an' mind."

"Oh," said Nor. He sipped from his cup. "Are you sure don't offer massages?"

"I know how to make muscle relaxers that'll make you feel like warm butter."

"I like her," Nor said to Ash.

Ash rolled her eyes. "You're in trouble, aren't you, Jak?"

"You protect me," said Jak, ignoring Ash's question. "I'll protect you and those you deem worthy from the ills that plague this mortal plane."

Ash considered Jak's proposal. She couldn't take it, or the fae, at face value. Fairies were tricky beings, and there was nothing they loved more than getting one over on their enemies. Or even their friends.

"I can help you find your souls, too."

Ash shook her head. "We live in Las Vegas. Finding souls isn't a problem."

"What's better?" asked Jak. "Going out to get your souls, or having 'em delivered?"

"Everybody loves take-out," agreed Nor.

Ash considered Jak's proposal. The problem with being a soul shifter, other than being the only one in existence, was that once she imbibed her first living essence, she had to take a soul every ninety days. She could take more, but not less, otherwise, she degenerated. She was immortal in the sense that she could live forever. But she was not indestructible. She could be killed.

Long ago, there had been more soul shifters. Their need to take essences and their ability to assume the forms of those whose souls were devoured absolutely terrified sentient beings. Human and parakind alike had deemed them evil and hunted every last one to extinction.

Supposedly.

Her existence was an anomaly.

Ash's gaze strayed to Jak, who waited patiently. Fairies weren't liars, but they knew how to bend the truth. She crossed her arms and narrowed her gaze. What was Jak's real angle?

"I can bake," said Jak.

Nor perked up.

Jak noticed Nor's sudden attention and immediately understood he was the weak link. The fairy went in for the kill. "Cupcakes, cream puffs, apple pies, chocolate cake, quiches, and the best waffles you've ever tasted."

"I'm drooling. Oh, let's keep her, Ash," said Nor. "Please?"

"Your word is your bond, soul shifter. Everyone knows that you never break a promise. Do we have a deal?"

"Hang on. What am I protecting you from?" asked Ash.

"Everything."

"For how long?"

Jak nibbled her lower lip. "The next hundred years."

"If I wanted to be stuck with someone for a hundred years, I'd marry a vampire."

Jak's laughter tinkled like tiny ringing bells. "I'm much better company than a *deamhan fola*."

"Oh, for fuck's sake." Ash took a big gulp of bourbon, appreciating the smooth burn that warmed her stomach.

"A hundred years," said Jak. "You protect me. I use my gifts to help you."

"The gift of baking, too, right? I want carbs, Ash." Nor fluttered his eyelashes. "I'm a werewolf with needs, you know."

Jak held out her hand. "Do we have a deal?"

"Those better be damned good waffles," she muttered, shaking the fae's hand.

Nor let out a "squeee" and hugged the fairy. "You're going to love Las Vegas."

BONUS MATERIAL #3
Deleted Scene with Rick Huntson

"**YOU AND YOUR** daughter should learn not to sneak up on people."

"Noted." He stared at her. She stared back. He broke eye contact first and let his gaze bounce around the scuzzy hotel room.

"Quite a place you got here."

"I don't do fancy."

Ash looked at the bed across from hers and saw Margaret asleep.

"You told Maggie that Sarah was dead."

"She asked me, I told her."

"Yeah, well, you just don't tell a kid that her mom's dead."

"I do a lot of things, Rick, but I don't lie." Ash got off the bed and stretched. Her pink jacket lay discarded on a nearby chair. The great thing about her jacket was that no one else could wear it. In fact, thanks to Bernie's spell work, most people were unconsciously repelled by it.

94

"What's the deal with your daughter, anyway?"

His gaze flicked away then returned. "What do you mean?"

"She can trigger spells and see what's beyond the senses of most humans."

His gaze was hard now. "You talk about magic like it's real."

"I didn't say magic. You did." She put on her jacket and grabbed her boots. "Why would demons attack your family?"

"Demons." Rick shook his head. "We were making dinner. Maggie had just finished her bath and was picking out a storybook. I smelled this … Jesus, I don't know … like something rotten. Something burning. Everything in the kitchen went wild. I heard maniacal laughter then the knives flew off the counter and…"

He didn't finish, but he looked devastated. Waking to a life ruined was a feeling she knew all too well.

Ash finished putting on her boots and opened the top dresser drawer to retrieve her weapons. As she loaded her belt with knives and two of her favorite guns, she said, "There's something about your little girl, Rick. They were after her." Ash knew the timing of her return to her old house and the attack on the Huntsons was not coincidental. She just didn't know why the demons would go after Margaret.

"Get the hell out of town. Whatever life you had here is over."

"Like yours, Natasha?"

"My name is Ash." So, he'd recognized her. Goody for him. "Stay off the grid. No credit cards, no ATMs, no cell phones, no contact with anyone. She pulled a glittering silver card out of another pocket.

"Contact this man, tell him I sent you. Kael owes me a solid. He'll get you and Maggie everything you need to start over."

"I can't believe this is happening."

"If you want to keep your daughter safe, you'll take my advice."

"Okay." He hesitated. "I'm sorry about your parents, but I'm glad you survived."

"If you want to call it that." Ash zipped up her jacket, suddenly aware of her lack of empathy at his loss. She stared at Rick for a moment. "I'm sorry about your wife."

The silence that stretched between them was filled with seven kinds of misery. She had spent so long shoving down her feelings, that a moment like this one felt like getting filleted by a dull knife. Ash turned toward the door.

Rick grabbed her arm and swung her around. "Where are you going?" There was almost a plea in the question.

She didn't know if it was his grief, his fear for his daughter, or the cute dimple in his chin, but imprudently she confessed, "That night at the party, I wanted to kiss you. I always regretted not doing it." With the heat of his hand still on her arm, she leaned in, closing the space between them, and pressed her lips to his.

Startled, he returned her kiss, but she knew his response wasn't about attraction or lost love or even about regret. It was anguish. It was the need for connection. It was, she supposed, penance.

When she stepped back, he looked so wounded that she wished she hadn't been so damned impulsive. The man had obviously loved his wife and grappled with her loss. Everything he knew was gone.

"Would it make you feel better to slap me?" she asked softly.

He laughed, and the darkness cleared from his eyes. "No, but thanks."

"Take care of yourself." Once again, she turned to go.

"I wish you wouldn't leave." His eyes cut to his sleeping daughter.

"The faster I get away from you, the better chances you have." Ash couldn't face the kid. The loss of her mother would either make Margaret stronger or break her completely. Ash bet on stronger. "Say good-bye to her for me."

"Natasha?"

She turned and looked over her shoulder.

Rick held up the business card. "Thanks."

She nodded. "Good luck."

THE WEREWOLF'S BRIDE
#1 in The Pack Rules Series

"I'M SO EXCITED," said Cacie Lynn. "Just think, Belle! I could be engaged tomorrow!" She twirled around, her pink waitress skirt flaring and showing off her tanned legs. She wore her blonde hair in a single, long ponytail. She shone like the sun, that one, a pretty girl with a pretty smile.

And an empty head.

Cacie was sweet, she really was, but she wasn't much of a thinker. Bless her heart. Barely eighteen-years-old, she hadn't known much outside of our little desert community. At least I'd gotten in a few months of nursing school before I'd had to come back. I'd almost escaped—from this desolate patch of lonely earth and the destined fate of eldest daughters. But then Carolyn had died and as my bloodline's next oldest female, I was obligated to return.

In Bleed City, Nevada, nothing was more important than family honor.

Cacie and I worked in the only diner in town, and town wasn't much. The Road House Grill joined the Gas 'N Go, Macpherson's General Store, Aunt Lila's Antiques, and the Bleed City Library as the sum total of occupied buildings. Our population hovered around 500 folks, give or take, and nearly all of us from families who'd lived in the area for generations. Bleed City was once a gold mining town—until the gold ran out and the miners moved on. Like so many of the ghost towns that populated the deserts of Nevada, Bleed City should've been left to rot and ruin.

Then the werewolves came.

The pact was made.

And that brings me right back to Cacie's misplaced excitement about a possible engagement. Near as I could tell, the werewolves didn't view courtship the same way humans did. They were ferocious and impatient. When it was time for the Choosing—every twenty years—a pack of young, full-of-themselves werewolves showed up, and Bleed City handed over their eldest daughters.

The pact that saved the town—the one that still held more than 150 years later—was simple enough. The werewolves protected its people, provided for every man, woman, and child so that no person would ever be without a roof over their heads or food in their bellies.

All we had to do was give them firstborn females for werewolf mating and breeding.

"I swear! You are such a Negative Nelly." Cacie clucked her tongue. "For heaven's sake, the alpha is looking for a mate. You know how often that happens?"

I shook my head.

"It's been sixty years." She let loose a dreamy sigh. "Marrying the alpha sure would be something, wouldn't it?"

All Cacie's talk of werewolf marriage was making me testy. Several us would be at the Choosing tomorrow, and my nerves were raw from thinking about it. "Lord-a-mercy! Werewolf this. Alpha that," I said. "Don't you have anything better to talk about it?"

"Hmph! Some of us are *grateful* for what God's handed us."

If she thought God had anything to do with her being a werewolf's barefoot-and-pregnant bride, she was even dumber than I thought.

"We need to get back to work, Cacie. Why don't you go scrub down the coffee maker?"

She sighed in the deeply profound fashion reserved for drama queens, and then flounced off. Thankfully, the brew machine was on the other side of the diner, so I wouldn't have to listen to anymore of her jawing.

I grabbed the cleaner and paper towels and started wiping down counters and tables. No one was in the diner tonight, not even old Mr. Sanders, who usually wouldn't go home until we did. I had to admit I was worried he hadn't shown up, but every so often he dealt with the gout and stayed home. I decided to check on him, though, after we closed up. I didn't have a car, not many of us did, but there was no crime in Bleed City, no lurching, sex-starved killers jumping out of bushes. So, we tended to walk. Everything in Bleed City was within five miles of everything else. It took time to get from here to there, but it was no real burden.

Thirty or so minutes later, we'd finished our chores and prepped everything for the morning shift. Cacie had kept her mouth shut the whole time, and I was grateful. Truth was, I was a big ol' anxious mess about the Choosing. They called us mates or wives or whatever, but it still sounded like slavery to me. And the kicker? Werewolves wanted their females as pure as the driven snow. That's exactly what a young virgin needed—some big, hairy man driving himself into her with his … his *penis*.

I felt myself blush to the roots of my hair. I was raised chaste and virginal, same as my sisters. Sex was not something we discussed—ever. My parents were good people with kind hearts. They also had firm rules about behavior. Going to nursing school had opened my eyes about human bodies, but I was still uncomfortable with the idea of physical intimacy. I'd been raised in such a staid and proper household, it was difficult to think about the word *sex* without wanting to throw myself at a Bible.

"Ready?" Cacie had changed into jeans, a T-shirt, and Nikes. She put on her hoodie and heaved her purse over her shoulder. She studied my hair, some of which had escaped its ponytail, and then dropped her gaze over my stained waitress dress. She even took three seconds to judge my shoes, which were comfortable, but ugly. "Are you crabby about the werewolves because you're afraid you won't get picked? It's not like you'll have to take a scruffer."

Scruffers were the weakest members of the werewolf pack. They had some uses, so they weren't outright killed, but it was rare that they merited mates. They had to settle for whatever scraps were handed to them by the stronger members—whether it was clothes or food or women.

I put on my jacket and stuffed my wallet into a pocket. Cacie walked out first. I switched off the lights and then followed her, turning briefly to lock the door.

"Are you?" she persisted as we stood outside.

"Am I what?"

She sighed as if she'd been talking Calculus to a four-year-old. "Are you afraid you won't get chosen?"

"I hope I don't."

Her eyes widened. "Don't say things like that, Arabelle Winton! I know you never expected to be part of the Choosing, but you're doing right by the town. By all of us."

Even though Cacie and I were only four years apart, I still felt like I was older, older than the whole world sometimes. I was exhausted, and all I wanted was a hot bath and a good night's sleep.

"Oh, I don't mean anything by it. Go on home, honey," I said. "I'll see you tomorrow."

"All right then. Bye, Arabelle."

"Bye." I watched her disappear down Main Street. I sighed. Despite the sturdiness of my shoes, my feet ached something fierce. The whole of me was bone-tired. Still, it would only take five minutes to make sure Mr. Sanders was okay.

I headed toward the Bleed City Library. Mr. Sanders had been the town librarian until arthritis and old age made the job too difficult. He still lived in the tiny cottage on the property, though. No one had the heart to make him move—not even the new librarian, Mr. Richards. He'd taken the room above Aunt Lila's Antiques rather than oust Mr. Sanders from his home.

The little house was eerily dark and still. I swear the hair on the back of my neck stood straight up as I approached. I stopped, studying the square structure to see what had raised my hackles, but after a moment of listening and watching, I had no proof to sustain my worry.

I stepped onto the porch and knocked on the front door.

If it were possible, the strange quiet deepened, and I felt my stomach squeeze with trepidation.

Then I heard a long, harsh moan.

"Mr. Sanders? It's Belle." I pounded on the door. "You all right? You need some help?"

Crash! Was that glass breaking? Had he dropped dishes or knocked over a table full of knick-knacks? Well, that was that. I figured politeness would have to be sacrificed to make sure the sweet old man wasn't hurt—or worse.

No one in Bleed City locked their doors. So I wasn't surprised when the knob turned easily in my hand. The door swung open and I inched inside, waiting for my eyes to adjust to the interior darkness.

"Mr. Sanders?" My voice came out a whisper. Fear chilled me from the inside out and goose bumps prickled my skin. I cleared my throat and tried again. This time my voice was stronger. "Mr. Sanders?"

I pressed my hand against the wall, feeling for a light switch. My fingers skittered over a picture frame. It fell off the wall and clattered to the floor. The sound exploded like thunder in the too silent house.

I froze. My heart thumped in my chest, so fast and so loud, I was sure people in the next county could hear it.

I sucked in a shaky breath. It did no good to let

fear rule my actions. Scared out of my wits or not, I needed to stop acting like such a ninny. My eyesight had adjusted, and complete blackness had given way to shadowy shapes. I edged away from the wall, holding my hands out as I moved forward.

"Mr. Sanders?"

My hands brushed against what I easily recognized as a lampshade. I felt my way under the flimsy material and around the base until my fingertips slid over the switch. I twisted it, and breathed a sigh of relief when dim, yellow light chased away the darkness.

I pressed a trembling hand to my chest and took in the destruction. Good lord. The living room looked like a dust devil had whirled through it. The recliner near the hearth was overturned, the bookshelves on either side were divested of treasures, and the tall, antique bric-a-brac cabinet on the far wall had met a terrible end. Its glass planes were shattered and the contents inside hadn't fared that much better.

My gaze dropped to the floor. I stared at the shredded books and busted objects. What had happened in here?

Then I saw Mr. Sanders's bare feet poking out from behind the couch.

Oh no! I hurried around the bulky piece of furniture and nearly lost my footing. I'd slipped in a widening pool of blood, blood that seeped from the gaping wound in poor Mr. Sanders's narrow chest.

It only took the briefest of moments for me shut away the horror of what I was witnessing. Rusty training kicked in, and though I knew it was useless, I still knelt down and felt his neck for a carotid pulse. Nothing. *Of course there was nothing!* The hole in the man's chest was the size of a bowling ball. I studied the cavity. His ribcage had been shredded and his flesh told the tale of claws and teeth. Worst of all, his heart was missing.

Horror filled me.

Werewolf.

Order Your Copy Today
www.lovemyshifters.com

THE BROKEN HEART SERIES

The Broken Heart Series

#1 I'm the Vampire, That's Why

#2 Don't Talk Back To Your Vampire

#3 Because Your Vampire Said So

#4 Wait Until Your Vampire Gets Home

#5 Over My Dead Body

#6 Come Hell or High Water

#7 Cross My Heart

#8 Must Love Lycans

#9 Only Lycans Need Apply

#10 Broken Heart Tails

#11 Some Lycan Hot

#12 You'll Understand When You're Dead

#13 Lycan on the Edge

Broken Heart Holidays

#1 Valentine's Day Sucks *(Valentine's Day)*

#2 Harry Little, Leprechaun *(St. Patrick's Day)*

#3 Some Lycan Hot *(Halloween)*

#4 Werewolf, Interrupted *(Groundhog Day)*

Broken Heart Worlds

#1 Cupid's Christmas

#2 Cupid's Valentine

ABOUT THE AUTHOR

Michele Bardsley is a New York Times and USA Today bestselling author of paranormal romance. When she's not writing sexy tales of otherworldly love, she watches "Supernatural," consumes chocolate, crochets hats, reads books, and spends time with her husband and their fur babies.

www.MicheleBardsley.com

43170914R00073

Made in the USA
San Bernardino, CA
15 December 2016